Pat Rhoads Mauser

RIP-OFF

Collier Books
Macmillan Publishing Company
New York

Collier Macmillan Canada
Toronto

Maxwell Macmillan International Publishing Group
New York   Oxford   Singapore   Sydney

to Mister Smith

First Collier Books edition 1990

Copyright © 1985 by Pat Rhoads Mauser

Collier Books
Macmillan Publishing Company
866 Third Avenue
New York, NY 10022

Collier Macmillan Canada, Inc.
1200 Eglinton Avenue East
Suite 200
Don Mills, Ontario M3C 3N1

Printed in the United States of America

1 2 3 4 5 6 7 8 9 10

A hardcover edition of *Rip-Off* is available from
Atheneum, Macmillan Publishing Company.

Library of Congress Cataloging-in-Publication Data

Mauser, Pat Rhoads.
Rip-Off / Pat Rhoads Mauser.—1st Collier Books ed.
p.   cm.
Summary: Ginger needs her new friend for protection at her new school,
but in return she is expected to be a party to shoplifting.
ISBN 0-02-044471-0
[1. Schools—Fiction.   2. Friendship—Fiction.   3. Shoplifting—Fiction.]
I. Title.
[PZ7.M44583Ri   1990]
[Fic]—dc20
90–31543   CIP   AC

RIP-OFF

To Kelsey
Good luck with your own
writing

Pat Rhoads Mauser

1995

1.

Ginger Wilson sat on the carpeted stairs, elbows resting on her knees, and fought back welling tears. In one hand she held the notice that she had read so many times she had it memorized.

"Due to overcrowding in some areas, the school board has voted to redistribute . . . ."

"Bull!" Ginger said out loud. "What they mean is bussing. I'm going to be bussed all the way downtown!"

She wadded the notice angrily in her fist. She had known there would be some transfers—everyone did—but Ginger had figured that, out of a thousand kids, the odds were in her favor.

She smoothed out the paper again. Maybe she had missed something.

"Your child has been reassigned to Alcott High School for the remainder of the academic year."

"Academic? That's a laugh. How can they do this to me?" Her parents were out on the patio with ten-year-old Mark, but Ginger spoke loudly enough for them to hear. "Everyone knows Alcott's the worst school in town. The kids are rowdy; that old brick building looks as if it was built during the Civil War. And I'll bet they won't have any decent art classes, either." Ginger looked expectantly toward the screen door, but no one seemed to notice her.

Anyway, the worst of this was, she wouldn't be with Paula. How could she survive her freshman year without a best friend?

If the schools were too crowded, why couldn't they bus the teachers around? Or the maps and textbooks? Her parents knew how Ginger hated doing new things alone.

"How will I ever get on the right bus?" she complained.

"What are you mumbling about?" Mrs. Wilson called finally.

"Oh, nothing!" Ginger got up and went to lean against the screen door. A light curl of smoke from the domed barbecue kettle rose and disappeared in the yellowing leaves of the maple tree. The aroma of roasting chicken reminded her that she'd been too upset to eat all day.

"Quit worrying, will you?" Ginger's mother was a pretty woman with Elizabeth Taylor eyebrows and a thin, straight nose. As she sat on the edge of the brick planter box, she shaded her eyes from the afternoon sun. "Look, you were only at Jefferson for a few weeks. Transferring is not the end of the world."

"Maybe not for you. You were a cheerleader in high school and had lots of friends. It's different for me. Why didn't anyone *ask* me if I wanted to be transferred?"

"It never works when you ask," her brother Mark explained simply.

Ginger raised her arms and dropped them again. "It's no use." At the thought of the injustice, a sob escaped from her throat.

4

"Think of it as an adventure," her father said. "I changed schools a lot when I was a kid, and it didn't hurt me a bit." He rubbed the bald spot on top of his head.

Her mother stood up and slid open the screen door. "Come on and help me set the table."

Ginger followed her.

"Why don't you tell me what's *really* bothering you, Ginger. An ivy-covered building, lots of trees, a beautiful fountain out front. . . ," she counted the points off on her fingers. "I should think an artist like you would appreciate—"

"Yeah, sure, I've heard all about that fountain. It's not exactly an art object, and I'll bet Alcott doesn't even have a pottery wheel." Ginger took a handful of silverware from the drawer and started laying out four places around the kitchen table.

"You can take pottery classes at the Y, if that's all you're worried about."

"Why couldn't they have sent those notices out during the summer? At least I would have a friend by now. I'll probably never see Paula anymore." She turned away from her mother and pushed her long brown hair away from her wet cheeks.

"So that's it. Paula." Her mother reached for her hand and patted it as if Ginger were a five-year-old. "Everything's going to be all right."

Her father came in with a heaping plate of crispy, golden chicken. Mark carried a bowlful of corn on the cob, each ear wrapped in foil.

"You're not crying again, are you?" Mr. Wilson looked at Ginger and then at his wife. A deep frown pulled at his eyebrows.

5

"Well, they throw the girls into the fountain." Ginger sniffed. "And ruin their clothes. Think of all that wasted money."

Her mother laughed. "Ginger, really. I'm sure that's just a story. Where did you hear a thing like that?"

"From Paula."

"Oh, from Paula. It must be true, then," her father said sarcastically. "Personally, I think separating the two of you is a good idea."

Ginger folded her arms. "Why?"

"So you can learn to think on your own."

I don't want to think on my own, Ginger started to say, then stopped herself. That didn't sound right. What she meant was, her life had been going along just fine. Now everyone wanted to undo it.

"The point is," her mother interrupted, "there's nothing we can do about the transfer, so we'll all have to make the best of it."

"We?" Ginger was indignant. "You mean me! *I'll* have to make the best of it . . . all by myself. You could make a stink and refuse to let me go." No one answered.

Mark looked up from under his blond bangs. "If they try to throw you in the fountain," he said, "you could always run."

Ginger sighed. Her brother was only in fourth grade and didn't understand anything. "No, I couldn't. They'd just catch me and then throw me in."

"I don't think you'll have any trouble," her mother said. "I have a feeling the boys are going to like you."

"Sure they are," her father insisted. "Take it from someone who used to be a boy. You're a very pretty girl."

"I am not."

"Of course you are," Her mother said. "You have lovely green eyes and a beautiful figure."

"She's got another zit," Mark pointed out.

Ginger's hand went to her chin, where an itchy red spot had appeared just since morning. "I hate boys anyway. Isn't there some way you can get me out of this?" she pleaded.

Her parents exchanged looks of exasperation and sat down at the table. Everyone started reaching for the food. Ginger was surprised to feel so hungry when her life was falling apart.

"We think you're one of the lucky ones," her father argued. "Forty students in one classroom is too much for any teacher to handle. At Alcott you'll have smaller classes. You'll probably love it, once you get used to it."

Nervously, Ginger worked a tiny piece off the edge of her paper napkin, rolled it between her fingers, and dropped it into her lap. "What if my clothes are all wrong?"

"Ginger." Her father held a fork in one hand and a knife in the other as he wound up for one of his famous lectures. "It wouldn't hurt to be a little different from the others. I'll never understand why you kids want to look like everyone else. My parents could never afford to buy me shetland sweaters or designer jeans and, as you can see, I've turned out just fine."

"Well, I. . . ."

"You're all sheep. If one of you were to jump over a cliff, I swear the rest would follow."

Whenever her father made this comparison, which was often, Ginger couldn't help seeing bloody sheep carcasses lying at the bottom of a cliff.

How was she supposed to answer that? she wondered.

And how was she to know? Did the kids at Alcott wear jeans? Or skirts and sweaters? Maybe they all wore dresses.

"Don't be a sheep," Dad persisted. "Make your own decisions."

Like which school to attend? Ginger wanted to ask. It was clear she couldn't talk to her parents about anything anymore.

2.

Ginger waited alone at the corner of Forty-ninth and Martial Way for the bus that was supposed to be coming in three minutes. She leaned against a light pole and considered the other corners coming together at the same intersection. Maybe she should be across the street in front of the hardware store.

Ginger's pantyhose rubbed together at the knees and the damp morning air swirled up under her dress. She pulled at the acorn print as if she could somehow make it longer.

I'll die if the girls are all wearing pants, she thought. But she had already changed twice: from jeans to slacks, to the brown acorn dress with the white collar. Better to be overdressed than under, she had decided. But now she wondered if the saying weren't the other way around: better to be underdressed. . . .

Ginger moved her elbows in and out several times, fanning her sticky armpits. If only she weren't so nervous. Her hair flopped against her forehead as she exhaled a puff of air. Whew! Relax, she commanded herself. After all, what can they do to you on the first day?

A minute later, two sophomore girls Ginger recognized from Jefferson approached the corner, both dressed in pants. With them was Lance Woodward in his usual hooded sweat shirt.

What's he doing here? Ginger wondered. Lance had made life miserable for Ginger since second grade, when he put a fat worm in her lunchbox. He was always in trouble, and he never seemed to take a bath.

But today brand-new jeans squeaked as he walked and, for once, his hair was cut; a white space showed around his ears. He must be transferring too, Ginger concluded.

"Hi." Ginger spoke to the girls, being careful not to look directly at Lance. Last year he had graduated to making fun of her any time she made a mistake, which was just about every time she was near him. He was probably already busy thinking up some smart-aleck remark for her.

"Hi," one of the girls answered. "You really look nice today."

"Oh . . . thanks. I decided to dress up for a change."

Lance grinned. "You going to Alcott?"

"No," Ginger said, beating him to the punch. "I got a job with a newspaper and I'm covering the bus stop." She looked away.

"Well, the *bus stop* is on the other side," Lance informed her. "Come on."

Ginger's face burned. "I know *that*," she answered quickly, "but I have to wait here— I'm allergic to the Scotch broom over there."

Lance turned and looked across the street. "It's not even blooming."

"I know," Ginger said, gesturing toward the green bush. "It's the leaves. They make me sneeze."

Lance hesitated. The two girls crossed the street. "Well, okay," he said and followed them.

Ginger ground her teeth together. Good going, she thought. Now I have to wait on the wrong corner all year.

When the bus finally rattled down the street, Ginger joined the others and stood in line looking up at the strange faces at the windows.

She climbed the steps and made her way to an empty seat near the back of the bus. A blond girl looked up as she passed. The popular type, Ginger decided. You could always tell by the snooty looks on their faces. Paula would sit down with a girl like that, but Ginger couldn't. Several other kids looked up. No one smiled.

Ginger settled into a seat and looked around. Every girl on the bus wore jeans. How was she supposed to have known that they'd all dress the same as Jefferson kids?

The smell of diesel fuel swam around her nose so that, by the time the long ride was over, her head throbbed. Ginger looked out the window at Alcott High School and at the kids who arrived from all directions.

A concrete woman with water spewing out of her head stood in the middle of the lawn to the right of the school. Louisa May Alcott. She stood in a fluted dish on one foot, and, as the water overflowed, it rained into a pool at the bottom. Curved concrete benches surrounded the fountain.

To Ginger's relief, no girls floundered in the pool. A

few sat on the benches with boys, but the scene was like a pretty painting. Maybe Mom had been right and the stories about the fountain were just tall tales.

Ivy grew all over the front of the red brick building, like mold spreading out over a piece of bread. It had been cut neatly away from the windows and big double doorway.

The bus crept ahead, then lurched to a stop, and the kids crowded off. Sounds of laughter mingled with the splashing of water.

For one insane moment Ginger looked for Lance, someone familiar, then quickly dismissed the idea. She was better off alone. She walked nervously toward the school, eyeing everyone she passed. Kids were gathered around the fountain talking, sitting on benches, and sprawled on the lawn nearby. One boy sat on the grass with his jeans rolled up, dangling his feet in the pool. Relaxed. Comfortable.

Alcott is kind of pretty, Ginger thought. She breathed deeply several times and turned her face toward the blue sky. A row of green-and-gold oak trees spanned the front of the school and various kinds of bushes grew next to the building. A hedge bordered the walk to the fountain.

A boy in glasses whistled at her as he rushed by.

Ginger laughed and let out her breath. Maybe it wouldn't be so bad, she thought optimistically. Maybe she could "make the best of it."

Her heart rate had almost slowed to normal when a shriek cracked through her thoughts. She jumped out of the way as a posse of boys dragged a red-haired girl across the sidewalk in front of Ginger. A smear of blue jeans and multicolored shirts rushed by.

Screaming girls scattered in all directions as boys

stampeded after them. Ginger stood in confused panic, wondering which way to go.

Hardly taking time to consider, she headed for the massive front steps of the school, but was cut off by a threesome of boys racing down the stairs two at a time. So instead, she crouched behind a bush, praying no one would notice her.

The red-haired girl kicked frantically but was no match for the five boys. They picked her up off the ground and waded into the pool, hoisting her above their heads into the dish at the base of Louisa May Alcott.

Ginger's throat went dry. They can't make me go to school here! I'll never survive in a place like this!

Water slopped out from under the girl's jeans as she sat helplessly screaming down at the boys.

"Get me off of here right now! Help! Someone help me!"

Ginger gaped as one girl after another was dragged into the water.

A boy with bushy black hair flew down the wide steps. "Stacy's on the fountain!" he screamed and ran so close to Ginger that she felt the morning air swish across her arm. She noticed a smile on the boy's face, as if something wonderful had just happened.

Ginger pressed herself into the bush and peered through the flat green leaves. Her heart pounded as if she had just run all the way to school instead of riding the bus.

Darkened tendrils of hair dripped over the girl's shoulders. White lace showed through a wet blouse that clung to her skin.

"Come on, you guys," the girl called with a laugh, changing her tactics. "Get me off of here. Please."

Ginger forced herself to walk calmly out from behind the bush. Then she leaped up the steps in three long strides. Her hand connected with the big, brass door handle, and a second later she stood in the front hall of Alcott High School.

Kids rushed back and forth, seemingly unaware of the circus going on outside. None of the girls wore dresses.

Lance was in the office and saw Ginger walk by. "Hey, we're in the same homeroom."

Being suddenly so alone, Ginger felt more friendly toward Lance than she had earlier. "We are? Where is it?"

Lance shrugged. "Second floor, I guess. You have to register first."

As he pushed past her, Ginger thought how funny Lance looked with his dark hair riding above his ears.

"Wait up," Ginger said. "We can look for it together."

Lance headed up some old wooden stairs to the right of the office. "I gotta stop in at the can," he said and disappeared into a mob of kids.

Ginger watched him. How does he know where the "can" is? she wondered.

Tables had been set up in the office for the new students. Ginger noticed green, yellow, pink, and blue cards lying in neat piles next to a box of pens and pencils. She chose a pink FRESHMAN card, filled it out, and handed it to a lady behind the counter. The woman checked her list.

"Okay, Ginger, you're in Homeroom 218. You'll be needing a gym outfit next week, but your teacher will tell you about that. And there's an ASB fee of eight dollars. Do you want to pay that today?"

"Um, no. I don't have enough money with me." Ginger

had already paid an ASB fee at Jefferson. Why couldn't they transfer that, too?

"Okay. Bring it as soon as you can."

"Where's Room 218?"

"Upstairs and to the right."

On her second full circle around the upstairs hallway, the bell went off, a loud blast that reverberated through Ginger's head. She walked faster: 216, 217, 219. Kids and teachers rushed past her in both directions. Little puddles of water followed several boys down the hall.

Finally, Ginger spotted 218 stenciled backward on the glass window of a door. She peeked in. This can't be right, she thought and checked the number once more.

There were no desks in the room, only long black counters with stools every five feet or so. Pipes and little hoses grew out of the back of each counter.

Lance had already claimed a stool in the third row, and when he saw Ginger, he reached over and patted the empty seat next to him.

No way, Ginger thought. I'll sit on the floor before I sit next to you!

3.

A man at the front of the room glanced at Ginger and beckoned for her to come on in. She blushed. He was very young with blue, blue eyes and tan face. Behind his head, on the chalkboard, the words, *Hi, I'm Mr. Clarke,* had been scrawled.

The students looked like normal freshmen; the girls in jeans and blouses, the boys in jeans and shirts. Ginger wriggled uncomfortably in her dress and stepped into the room.

Immediately her nose burned with a terrible smell.

The teacher suddenly jumped up and sniffed, too. "All right!" he boomed. "Some wise guy has the gas on!"

Ginger froze. Kids swiveled on their stools to see who might have turned on the gas. Mr. Clarke left his desk and walked slowly down the first aisle, stopping to sniff the air every few feet.

Ginger scanned the class. Lance moved his fingers across the counter and quietly tightened the faucet in front of him. It figures, Ginger thought. The teacher didn't seem to notice, but when he came to Lance, he stopped abruptly.

"Are you a wise guy?"

"No." The white space on Lance's neck reddened.

"Good, because I don't like wise guys. What's your name?"

"Lance Woodward."

"Mis-ter Wood-ward!" The teacher folded his arms and smirked. "There's an interesting experiment I'd like you to do for us."

Ginger crept the rest of the way into the room and sat down on the nearest empty stool, praying the movement would not catch the teacher's attention.

"Open your drawer and take out some matches," he ordered.

Lance did as he was told, and everyone in the room seemed to swallow at once. A small blond girl in the front row looked back and smiled on one side of her mouth.

"Now, *if* your gas had been on and you were to light a match. . . . Go ahead, Woodward, light it!"

Lance just sat there.

"What's the matter, Woodward?"

Lance took a match out of the box and closed it, then held it ready to strike.

Ginger wanted to cover her head but was afraid to move. Would the whole room blow up? she wondered.

"LIGHT IT!"

Lance jumped, and tears suddenly shone in his eyes.

"LIGHT IT!" the teacher bellowed again and rocked on his heels, waiting.

"I can't." Lance's voice quivered. "I . . . accidentally . . . turned on the gas."

"Then you're a wise guy."

"Yeah . . . I guess so."

The other kids in the room started to laugh. Mr. Clarke ignored them as he stared at Lance for a long minute. Then he returned to the front of the room.

"For the benefit of the transfer students, another wise guy has just been initiated into homeroom. Anyone can be initiated. All you have to do is turn on the gas or mess with my chemicals. Is that clear?"

Ginger nodded along with the rest of the class, carefully looking straight ahead to avoid eye-contact with Lance. As far as she was concerned, she'd never seen him before.

"Will you new people raise your hands so I can assign lockers?"

Three hands went up; Lance's, another boy's, and Ginger's.

"Doylita, you're going to have to share your locker."

The blond girl in the front row jumped off her stool

16

and stood with her hands on her hips. She was at least a head shorter than any ninth-grader Ginger had ever seen, with long, silky hair that swished across her back.

"I have to have a locker by myself!" she exploded. "I can't get all my stuff into *half* a locker."

"Sorry. You're the only girl in the room who doesn't have a partner."

"We'll see about that," the girl said under her breath.

Lance and the other boy were paired off in a locker next to the supply room.

"Ginger Wilson, you'll be sharing locker number 287 with Doylita Willard. She'll show you how to work it."

"Over my dead body," Doylita mumbled, and the girl next to her snickered.

Ginger looked at the back of the blond head, but Doylita did not turn around. Ginger's chest ached. Doylita seemed to hate her before they even met. Well, I don't like you either, Shorty, she wanted to yell at her.

Mr. Clarke handed out schedules to the new students, and, to Ginger's surprise, her classes were practically the same as the ones she'd had at Jefferson, except in different order. Instead of pottery, though, she was going to have Basic Design.

Ginger looked at the clock. In five minutes she would have to find her first class. Nervously, she tore pieces off a sheet of notebook paper and rolled them into little scrolls in her lap. Then, too soon, everyone stood up and headed for the door. Ginger checked her schedule again with sudden panic. Her first class was English in Room 104.

She watched Doylita pick up a book bag and slide off her stool. As the girl turned toward her, Ginger saw the most perfect doll's face she had ever encountered.

Heart racing, she tried to rush after her, but Doylita had already melted into the mass of kids going out the door.

A boy crowded in behind Ginger and leaned toward her ear. "I almost blew it . . . so to speak," Lance tried to explain with a weak laugh.

"I don't know you," Ginger whispered, then slipped through the mob and headed down the hall toward the stairs. On the way she passed Doylita standing at one of the lockers.

"Hey," Doylita called, "come here."

Ginger obeyed and made her way to the outside of the noisy hallway.

"Look, it's not your fault about the locker. Do you want to put your stuff in here for now?"

Ginger smiled down at her with relief. "I don't really have anything yet."

Doylita stepped up into the locker in order to reach a shelf on top. "I have a mirror and a comb up here," she said. "Can you bring anything?" She hopped down and drew her mouth up into a one-sided smile.

The bottom of the locker was a mess of little things still bearing price tags: lip gloss, a thermometer hooked to a card, a new scarf, and a blister pack of thumbtacks. Doylita was already well-supplied. Why did she need a thermometer? Ginger wondered. "How about a box of Kleenex?"

"Okay, but remember this is *my* locker, so I'm in charge." A dark fringe of eyelashes surrounded her beautiful blue-green eyes. Her face glowed a soft peach color.

"Yeah, sure. Thanks."

"The combination is R 6-L 17-R 20. Remember that! Let's see your schedule." Doylita grabbed it out of her hand. "Oh, good. We have all but two classes together. Come on."

Ginger followed her. "Did it take you long to get used to this place?" she asked, as they made their way down the stairs. Kids pushed forward eight abreast, squeezing Ginger against the wall.

Doylita grinned. "Not when you've been around Alcott as much as I have."

Ginger wondered what she meant. Doylita *was* a freshman, wasn't she?

The girls burst through the door to 104 into a quiet room and sat down in the back row.

"And they said Jefferson was overcrowded! That's a laugh," Ginger mumbled. As the kids filed in, she counted thirty-eight students, only two less than the forty her parents had complained about.

Between third period and lunch, Doylita led Ginger back to their locker. Doors clanked open and closed in a metallic roar that filled the hallway. Kids pushed each other against the lockers and shouted to friends passing by.

"Here we are." Doylita stopped in front of the beige-colored locker. A long scratch ran the length of the door. "Why don't you open it this time."

Ginger looked down at the padlock. "The doors locked automatically at Jefferson."

"Then watch me." Doylita twirled the knob on the front of the lock first one way and then the other. She didn't even try to move it slowly so Ginger could see what she was doing. Then she gave a yank, and the lock opened. "When you've opened ten million of these, like I have, it's a snap," she announced and squeezed the lock shut again. "Now you try it."

Ginger had already forgotten the combination. R 6-L something? She turned the knob back and forth as Doylita had done, thinking maybe she'd get lucky, but nothing happened.

"What are you doing?" Doylita took the lock from Ginger. "The combination is R 6-L 17-R 20," she said, sounding annoyed.

"Oh, yeah, I forgot." Ginger took a pencil and wrote the combination on the cover. "Let me try again."

"We don't have time now," Doylita said. "We'd better get to the lunchroom if we want anything to eat."

Ginger looked around her at the chaos and at the crowd of kids she didn't know. Even the pinkish color of the walls looked strange.

Gratefully she followed her new locker partner downstairs to the lunchroom. Thank goodness Doylita knew her way around.

Doylita led Ginger straight downstairs to the cafeteria. She knew exactly what to do. "Stick with me," she hollered over the noise. "I know someone at the head of the line."

The sounds of dishes rattling, silverware clanking, and kids yelling mingled into one deafening roar. Long tables and benches filled the room, with hardly any space to walk between. Kids climbed over each other and squeezed into any niche they could find.

"Hey, Corine," Doylita shouted.

A pretty girl with dark brown hair and brown eyes turned around and motioned for Doylita to cut in front of her. Ginger followed, feeling the disapproving eyes of the other kids all the way to the head of the line.

"Are you sure it's okay to do this?" Ginger asked.

"It's okay. Corine's a senior."

"Oh," Ginger said. She had been at Jefferson long enough to understand the implication. Juniors and seniors did anything they wanted.

Doylita took a tray and reached for the silverware. "Corine, this is my new locker partner." She turned to Ginger. "What did you say your last name was?"

"Wilson."

"Ginger Wilson, this is Corine," Doylita said. "She's a cheerleader."

"Really? That's great," Ginger said.

Corine smiled. How did Doylita know a senior cheerleader? Ginger wondered.

The three girls carried their trays to the back of the cafeteria, holding them over the heads of the kids who were already gulping their food.

A girl looked up at Doylita as she passed with her tray. "Hi, Doyle. Have a seat," she said. She pulled in her elbows as a big girl in a glittery T-shirt squeezed in next to her.

A boy tumbled off the end of the bench. "Hey, knock it off," he yelled, steadying his tray.

"I don't think there's enough room for all of us," Doylita said.

Ginger laughed. "I should take a picture of this for my mother."

"What?" Corine asked.

"Oh, nothing."

Doylita jabbed Ginger in the back with her tray. "Hurry, let's grab those spaces by the apple machine."

Ginger allowed herself to be pushed along while she talked over her shoulder to Corine. "It's just that I was transferred here because of overcrowding at Jefferson."

"You're kidding."

Doylita jabbed Ginger again. "If you don't shut up," she snapped, "we'll lose our places."

Shut up yourself, Ginger wanted to say. The girls hurried and slammed their trays down just as a couple of black kids did the same thing. Ginger looked around for another space, but Doylita ignored the kids and stepped over the bench to sit down.

Corine did the same, and Ginger followed. She wiggled her shoulders, trying to claim a space on the crowded bench, and found herself wedged up next to one of the biggest boys she'd ever seen. His broad, muscular shoulders were hunched over a tray of spaghetti and peas.

"Hey, Doyle, baby!" he said, when he noticed Doylita. "How's it goin'?"

"Not too shabby," Doylita answered. "I nearly got blown up in homeroom."

"Oh, that's right. You're in Clarke's chemistry lab, aren't you?"

"Yep."

Ginger looked at Doylita in awe. Did she really know this guy? He had to be a senior, and *so cute.*

The boy rocked with laughter. "You mean someone turned on the gas again?"

"You got it," Doylita said. "Some new kid."

Ginger cringed.

More laughter followed as the blond boy elbowed a fuzzy-haired boy sitting next to him. "Doyle's got Clarke for homeroom."

"Is that right? Well, stay out of the man's chemicals, whatever you do."

"It happens every year," someone else put in, "but so far no one has lit the match."

Soon everyone at the table, except Ginger, was laughing and into the conversation. What would happen, they wondered, if someone called Clarke's bluff?

Three kids finished eating and left. Three more took their places.

"Oh, hi, Doylita," one of the newcomers said. "Anyone dumped you in the fountain yet?"

"Nope, and they'd better not try it."

"Wintermeyer will probably get mad and have it turned off, like the old principal last year.

"I hope so," Ginger said quietly.

Pale blue eyes looked down at her. "Hey, Doyle, who's your friend?" the boy asked.

Doylita reached up to drape an arm around Ginger's shoulder. "This is my locker partner, and I want you guys to leave her alone, okay? Ginger Wilson; Rol Swenson."

"Hi." Ginger blushed and concentrated on her food; spaghetti with a greasy piece of French bread and a peach half. The orange blur ran together in front of her eyes. Her muscles tightened as Rol patted her shoulder.

"Any friend of yours is a friend of ours," he said.

Ginger smiled, being careful to keep her lips tightly closed. Spaghetti seemed to expand inside her mouth until she nearly gagged.

An uncomfortable quarter hour later, she and Doylita headed back upstairs for afternoon classes: art, science and P.E.

In the art room, Ginger was surprised to discover a stack of old wooden easels leaning against the back wall. They'd never had easels at Jefferson. A small surge of excitement grabbed her as she picked out one of the least paint-encrusted ones for herself.

After general science with Mr. Clarke and a sweaty game of basketball in P.E., Ginger raced back up the stairs behind Doylita to turn in her schedule and return to their locker.

Glancing out the window at the end of the hall, she saw that the sky was a brilliant blue. If she were at Jefferson she could be home and into her jeans within a few minutes. Instead, she faced a long bus ride, and the bus stop was on the far side of the school, past the fountain.

Once again Doylita took charge of opening the locker, as if it were her personal property.

"Everyone goes down to the stores after school," Doylita said, stepping up into the locker for her books. "Why don't you come along?"

"I have to catch the bus," Ginger explained.

Doylita gave her hair a flip. "No problem," she said. "You can take the city bus later. It's only twenty-five cents for students. Do you have a quarter?"

"Well, yes, but . . . ," Ginger hedged. This might be a safe way out of the school, but she was sure her mother expected her home soon, especially on her first day at a new school. "I really should get home. Besides, I don't have any extra money to spend downtown."

"That's okay," Doylita said, jumping down from the locker. "I just look at things." She giggled and leaned closer. "Or rip them off."

Doylita grinned on one side of her mouth. Her perfect little face glowed with innocence, and Ginger shook her head in a quick double take.

"You what?"

5.

"Just kidding," Doylita answered quickly. "Do you want to go, or not?"

Ginger's gaze moved to the bottom of the locker that was littered with new merchandise. "I'd better get home."

But before she even pushed open the big front doors of the school, she heard screaming from the front lawn and knew what was going on; some poor girl was in the fountain again.

She stopped outside at the top of the steps. The sky, crisp and blue, hung like a satin robe behind the green-and-gold leaves of the oak trees. Water droplets from the fountain bounced like little jewels in the sun.

Except for the two girls trapped on the top of Louisa May, the picture was a perfect watercolor. Ginger looked on with disgust and her chest tight with dread, but some morbid fascination kept her eyes on the scene.

An Oriental girl sat in the pool at the bottom of the fountain with books and papers floating around her.

Another girl stood dripping wet, pouring water out of her shoe. One of the two girls on top of the statue was crying. Boys ran wild, snatching more victims.

Doylita leaned over the ledge, grinning as if she were enjoying the show. How did she know they wouldn't get her next?

"This is horrible," Ginger said. "Where's the principal? Doesn't he care?" She looked back toward the doors. Should she report this? How was she going to get home?

Doylita's face went into a quick scowl and then she smiled again. "It's no big deal. It's a warm day. I just might take a dip myself." She flounced down the stairs, as if she didn't have a thing to worry about.

Ginger hesitated, then followed her. No one came near them except to say, "Hi, Doyle." "Hey, Doyle, how's it goin'?" It was as if they were walking in a protective bubble.

A few yards away, a tall, skinny boy picked up a girl and packed her, kicking and screaming, over his shoulder to the fountain. His clothes were already drenched, as if this were his second or third trip.

Ginger stopped, afraid to go any further, and considered what to do. Something crawled inside her stomach. Doylita might have a lot of friends, but they wouldn't care if some Jefferson girl got drenched. Ginger glanced at the yellow buses lined up at the far end of the school grounds.

"I suppose I could walk downtown," she decided quickly. "I guess my mother won't mind if I'm a little late. Are you sure I can get home on the city bus?"

Doylita's lip curled into a satisfied grin. "Of course I'm sure. They run every half hour."

The two girls turned away from the school and joined

a migration of kids heading downtown. Some followed in cars and hollered out the windows at the kids who were walking.

Ginger's feet burned in her heeled shoes, but she hurried along beside her locker partner, who skipped down the sidewalk.

The crowd headed for Freman's, the nicest department store downtown. Ginger had been there before with Paula or her family, but never with a whole mob of kids. She felt uneasy as the doors zipped open and she followed Doylita inside.

Already crowds of kids milled around in the aisles, picking up knickknacks and pulling at clothes. A book bag swung from nearly every girl's arm.

Mom would hate this, she thought, watching the kids swarm through the store, touching everything. Ginger noticed a group of girls looking at gauzy negligees, yanking them by the sleeves and holding out the long skirts.

"This is what I want for my honeymoon," one of the girls said. She looked no older than fourteen, a freshman. The gown floated on its hanger like a pink cloud.

Doylita stopped at a glass-topped counter and poked her finger into a tiny jar of red gloss, then dropped her bag of books on the floor and stepped up on it. She looked at herself in the mirror and rubbed the gloss on her lips. When she turned around, she looked as if she'd been eating cherry Popsicles.

"Try some," she offered, hopping down from her books. "It's okay, they're just samples."

A tall, blond salesgirl appeared on the opposite side of the counter. She wore a silky blue blouse, and her hair was coiled elaborately on the top of her head. Her face was flawless, with peach blush and blue eyeshadow.

She smiled at the girls. "Can I interest anyone in a free make-over?"

Ginger looked at Doylita. Free? What was the catch?

Corine, who was standing behind them said, "Why don't you go ahead, Ginger? We've all had it done."

Ginger looked at her watch. "I don't know. How long does it take?" But before she was able to protest much, she was sitting on a stool with a plastic cape over her shoulders.

"My name is Sherry," the salesgirl said. She tilted Ginger's chin. "Hm, nice bone structure."

Ginger sat very still, allowing Sherry to examine her face and wishing there were some way to hide the zit on her chin.

Doylita and the other girls stood off to the side to watch. Ten or twelve had gathered. Thank goodness most of the boys had moved on.

Sherry brought out a whole tray of make-up in beautiful bright bottles and tubes.

A warm fluorescent light shone down on them as the salesgirl pinned Ginger's hair back and went to work. First she applied a thin layer of tawny base make-up, then contouring blush in a soft shade of brown. Pink blush went above that.

"Your features are exquisite," Sherry said. "You should always wear a little make-up."

"Yeah, you look great," Doylita agreed.

Ginger smiled into a mirror on the counter. Her mother had offered to help her with make-up, but Ginger had never wanted to bother with it before.

Next Sherry brushed on three shades of eyeshadow: gray, then green and blue, which she blended outward toward Ginger's temples, giving her eyes an almond shape.

"Ooh," Corine sighed. "You look so . . . mature."

Mascara and a little eyebrow pencil finished her eyes, and Ginger blinked at herself. The girl in the mirror looked so different.

Sherry laughed. "I'll bet you didn't know how pretty you are." She finished up by running a cool fingertip with pink gloss along Ginger's lips. "There, what do you think?"

"I don't believe it's me. Thanks."

While Sherry was cleaning up the mess, she handed Ginger a sheet of paper.

The catch, she thought.

"Here's a list of products I used on you. You might consider investing in a few things at a time."

Ginger looked at the paper. Everything was so expensive.

"Remember, my name is Sherry, and I'm always here to answer your questions."

"Is that all there is to it?"

Sherry had already turned to two ladies who had just shown up. "Can I interest either of you in a free make-over?"

Ginger walked away with her locker partner, sneaking peeks at herself whenever she passed a mirror.

"You really do look great," Doylita assured her several times. She stopped at the opposite side of the make-up counter and opened a brand new tube of mascara.

"Let's go, "Ginger said nervously.

Doylita flipped her hair over her shoulder and pulled her mouth into a sneer. "You're really a goody-goody, aren't you? They don't care if we try a few of these things. How else are we going to know if we want to buy them?"

Ginger followed her to the next counter. Doylita had a point. They probably didn't care. But near the escalator, Doylita turned quickly and dropped a small brown case into her pocket. A price tag was stuck right on the front, and Ginger knew she had just ripped it off.

Ginger stared. She had never seen anyone steal anything before. "We just look at things, or rip them off," Doylita had said. She hadn't been kidding at all. Ginger looked at the floor. Someone ought to tell, she thought, but not me. A vague dizziness came over her like the time she'd seen a stiff, dead cat behind the grocery store.

"Come on," Ginger said more forcefully. "Let's go."

Doylita patted her pocket. "What's the matter?"

Ginger stepped on the escalator. "I . . . want to look at some shoes."

Corine and her friends rejoined them and the entire group rode the escalator to the second floor.

The shoe department was on the opposite side of the store near the down escalator. The first thing Ginger saw was a huge cardboard shoe displaying little yarn balls in various colors: green and yellow, red and white, and blue and gray.

"Oh, look!" Ginger reached over and squeezed a pair of red-and-white ones. "Jefferson colors." A gulp of homesickness caught in her throat.

"Hey, you're going to Alcott now. Our colors are green and yellow." Doylita pulled a pair of the pompons off the shoe.

"They're darling," a blond girl said as she bent down to hook a pair into her shoelaces, and with sudden inspiration she added, "Hey, Doyle, your dad will love these. Let's each get a pair and wear them to school tomorrow."

Why would Doylita's dad care about pompons? Ginger wondered. Her own father would think they were silly.

"Hey, yeah," several others echoed.

In a moment almost every pair of green and yellow pompons were gone, leaving little holes in the cardboard. The girls lined up at the cash register, including Doylita.

"Aren't you going to get any, Ginger?" A black girl named Mindy asked.

"Come on, get some pompons," Doylita coaxed. "They'll be gone in a couple of days, and then you'll be out of luck."

"Well, I don't have enough money right now."

"So . . . ?" Doylita grinned in a sly way, and Ginger knew exactly what she was suggesting.

"Want me to get some for you?" she whispered.

"No!" Ginger swallowed hard and looked back at the cardboard shoe. She had known Alcott kids were terrible. Why hadn't anyone believed her?

6.

Ginger's skin prickled with nervousness. "Maybe to-night," she hedged. "My dad might lend me the money." Fat chance, she knew.

By the time the group left the store, pompons bobbed on every pair of shoes except Ginger's. They really did look cute, even if they were the wrong color. Ginger pulled at her short dress. Her pantyhouse rubbed together like corduroy jeans. She had never felt so out of place in her life. Even her new make-over failed to cheer her up any longer.

When Ginger got home, her mother was waiting for her on the front porch, arms folded across her chest.

"Where in the world have you been?" she started in. "I've been worried about you. I thought you might have gotten confused and missed your bus."

"I'm sorry," Ginger said. "I took the city bus from Freman's. I didn't mean for you to worry."

"The city bus? Why?" As she spoke, Mrs. Wilson examined Ginger's face but didn't say anything about the make-up.

"I told you those stories about the fountain were true." Ginger went into the house and flopped down on the couch. Her mother followed her. "Practically every girl in the school got thrown in today," she exaggerated.

Mrs. Wilson glanced at Ginger's clothes.

"Not me. I went downtown with my new locker partner so I wouldn't have to walk past the fountain."

"You shouldn't have to do that! Why hasn't someone told the principal?"

"He already knows," Ginger answered, "but he's new, and there's probably nothing he can do about it."

A dark eyebrow raised. "I doubt that, Ginger."

"You should see those kids! Someone almost blew up my homeroom this morning!" She didn't mention that the culprit had been Lance Woodward from Jefferson. "Alcott kids are terrible. They shoplift, too."

"All of them?"

"Well. . . ."

"That doesn't mean *you* have to." She sounded just like Ginger's father.

"Well, I'm never going to like it at Alcott. I'm so different. And everyone carries book bags, canvas ones with pictures on them."

"That doesn't sound like such a big problem. You could whip up a book bag on the sewing machine in thirty minutes."

"Not like these." Ginger sighed. She didn't want solutions, she just wanted *out*! "You should see how crowded the lunchroom is, and there are thirty-eight kids in my English class. With all those transfers, Alcott is probably overcrowded now."

"Ginger, really!" She looked again at her daughter's face. "Where'd you get the make-up?"

"I had a free make-over at Freman's. Do you like it?"

"They did a nice job, but you look so . . . sophisticated."

Ginger smiled.

Later, at dinner, the tales of her first day at Alcott and the fountain were relayed to her father.

"What you're saying," Mr. Wilson scoffed, "is that the *kid*s run the school. Maybe I ought to call your principal."

"Dad, please!" Ginger cringed. "I'll be drowned if anyone finds out who complained."

"Maybe the boys are just getting carried away with the excitement of the new transfer students," Mrs. Wilson offered.

Mark laughed. "It's the girls who are getting carried away. Get it . . . carried away to the fountain?"

Only Mom laughed at the joke.

"I really hate Alcott," Ginger mumbled.

Her father leaned toward her. "Look, we have to give it a chance. If you're having problems, I'll call the principal. That's why he's there."

By the time Ginger figured out that she was stuck at Alcott and had worked up the courage to ask her dad about some pompons and a book bag, her napkin lay in a mound of tightly rolled bits in her lap.

"They're only three dollars, and they're really cute," she said of the pompons. Ginger had decided not to mention the part about not liking the colors; that would complicate matters. "And think how convenient a book bag would be."

Her father pushed his empty plate aside and leaned his elbows on the table. "What are these pompons made of? What do they do?"

"They're made of yarn, I guess," Ginger answered. "They don't *do* anything . . . except look cute." She wiped her hands on her jeans and her shredded napkin snowed on the floor. She looked down at the speckles. Why did Dad have to make everything so difficult? She hadn't even mentioned the fact that she was going to need a new gym outfit. Some girls would have asked for everything at once.

"I'll tell you what," he said, as if he were about to make her a great bargain. "I can see that a book bag would be a nice thing to have. I'll drive you downtown after dinner, but you'll have to save up for the pompons. Okay?"

Ginger forced a smile. If she had a choice between pompons and a book bag, she'd take the pompons, but she didn't seem to have a choice. "Doylita's bag has pictures of Ziggy on it."

Mark started to laugh. "Doylita. What a name!"

Ginger ignored her brother's remark. "May I be excused now? I've got to call Paula."

"Clear your plates," her father reminded her. He had gone all through dinner without noticing her make-over.

Ginger stacked her dishes in the dishwasher and went to the upstairs telephone. Good ol' Paula. At least she still had a best friend after school. The phone rang four, five, six times. No answer. Ginger hung up and dialed again. Still no answer.

She had so much to tell her; about the fountain, the chemistry lab, Doylita, the blond boy at lunch and, of course, her brand new make-over that everyone said made her look older. Paula had been into make-up since she was twelve and would probably be over in a flash to check Ginger out. If only she were home.

7.

Ginger watched intently for the bus, again on the wrong side of the street. What a mess she'd gotten herself into, telling Lance she was allergic to Scotch broom. But at least she was wearing jeans today—heavy, secure denim covering her legs. And she carried a brand-new book bag, white canvas with pictures of Garfield on the front.

She had tried her best to duplicate the make-up that Sherry had applied the day before and wondered if anyone would notice the difference. Probably not, since she knew almost no one at Alcott.

This morning Lance slouched against a utility pole and talked to the two girls who stood at the bus stop with him, but Ginger knew he was watching her, probably laughing to himself. Finally, he yanked off a small branch of Scotch broom and put it under his nose.

"It doesn't even smell," he hollered across the street.

"Yeah, I know," Ginger said. "It . . . gives off non-smelling fumes."

"Come on. You're not really allergic to anything."

"I most certainly am!" Ginger insisted, and it was true. She *was* allergic to some kind of mold, so she hadn't really lied.

A minute later the bus rumbled around the corner, barely giving Ginger enough warning to get across the street.

She looked at the Scotch broom and then at Lance. "I sure wish they'd cut that stuff down," she said, giving her tale one last shot of realism. The only thing to do now was play out the lie for the rest of the school year, maybe all through high school. She hated Lance for making her do this.

Ginger worked her way to the back of the bus and sat next to a girl she recognized from her P.E. class. Lance followed and sat directly in front of them.

Wire-frame glasses rested on the girl's freckled nose, and one thick brown braid hung over her shoulder.

"Hi," the girl said. "Aren't you in one of my classes?"

"Yeah. P.E." Ginger sat quietly for several blocks. "How do you like Alcott so far?"

"All right, I guess," the girl said. "Except for that stupid fountain. I liked Fairview a lot better."

"I transferred from Jefferson. My name's Ginger Wilson. What's yours?"

"Shelly Franklin."

The bus bounced along the road, stopping occasionally to pick up a huddle of kids.

"My dad might be calling to complain about the fountain today. You didn't get thrown in, did you?" Ginger felt herself go clammy at the thought.

"Almost. But every time a boy came near me, I spit at him. I'm real good at spitting. My record is seven feet."

The two girls snickered and, in front of them, Lance's shoulders bumped up and down.

He's listening to everything we say, Ginger thought. If only she had her paints, she'd reach up and fill in that white space below his hair with brown. Ginger smiled at the idea.

"Whose homeroom are you in?" Shelley asked.

"I have Clarke."

"Oh," she said. "He's so-o cute. I have Liddy, next to the cafeteria. Is it true that someone almost blew up the chemistry lab yesterday?"

Again Ginger looked at the back of Lance's neck. His ears wiggled with the strain of listening.

"Uh-huh. One of the boys turned on the gas."

"What a moron." Shelly laughed.

Lance slid down in his seat until only the top of his dark hair was visible.

"What's with him?" Shelley whispered.

"He's the moron."

The girls looked at each other and burst into fits of wild laughter, while Lance slid even further down in his seat. Finally he slipped all the way off onto the floor.

Ginger pretended not to notice. "Just ignore him," she whispered. "Tell me," in a louder voice, "do you have a locker partner?"

Shelley touched the bridge of her glasses to push them back into place. "Yeah, my cousin Doreen. I was really lucky. We have the same last name, so we ended up in homeroom together."

"Where is she?"

"She's a walker."

Lance pulled himself back up into his seat and turned toward Ginger with an embarrassed smirk.

"Will you stop listening to everything I say?"

Lance started to comment, then closed his mouth and looked from one of Ginger's eyes to the other. "What's all that gunk on your eyelashes? It looks like spiders are trying to crawl out."

"That's gross!" Shelley wailed.

Ginger raised her book bag to hit him, but when she did, pencils, pens, and a notebook slid out. She was still picking them up when the bus stopped in front of Alcott.

Shelley stood up and hurried toward the front. "There's Doreen," she said. "I've got to catch her. See you in P.E., Ginger."

"Yeah. See ya." Ginger stepped off the bus behind Lance.

The fountain gurgled happily as if it didn't know what had happened the day before. Several kids sat on the benches near the pool. Without a girl perched on top of her, Louisa May looked rather pretty, Ginger thought. One gray hand held a pen and the other an open book, as if she were writing a novel right there in the fountain.

Shelley and her cousin Doreen walked on ahead. Ginger scanned the school grounds for Doylita, feeling suddenly lonely. She was nowhere in sight, but Ginger noticed several pair of green-and-yellow shoe poms bobbing on the toes of Doylita's friends.

Spray from the fountain dampened Ginger's forehead as she approached the concrete benches.

Lance turned around, offering Ginger his arm. "May I escort you safely to your homeroom, damsel," he said with a slight bow.

"Are you kidding?" Ginger checked the water splashing off Louisa May's skirt, raining steadily into the pool. "I can't trust you! You'll escort me right into the moat!"

Lance twisted his mouth into a pained frown. "Then your safety is entirely out of my hands," he said, with a sweep of his arm.

"I'm quite capable. . . ."

Before Ginger could finish her sentence, someone grabbed her roughly from behind. Her brand-new book bag and its contents of pencils, combs, paper, and books scattered to the lawn as she struggled against him. Lance watched calmly.

"Help!" Ginger's face drained and her heart felt as if it would jump right out of her blouse. "Do something, you creep!"

Lance smiled and walked off.

Ginger tripped over her books as the boy pushed her across the lawn toward the fountain.

"My mom will kill me if I get my shoes wet!" Ginger screamed as she fought to free her arms. The boy smelled like tomato soup.

"You stink!" she yelled. "Get your filthy hands off me!"

He laughed and tightened his grip. Ginger clawed at the big fists that were locked around her waist.

"You stupid, idiotic moron! You slimy, imbecilic toad!" Ginger screeched every word she could think of. "Let me go right this minute, or you'll be sorry!"

Cold spray from the fountain blew into her face as the boy pushed her toward the concrete rim.

"I can't swim!" she pleaded.

"I've really got a wild one," the boy called to his friends. "Give me a hand."

Ginger held her breath and prepared to get drenched. She could almost feel the cold water on her feet when someone yelled, "Buzz off, jerk!"

Ginger opened her eyes to see a tall boy with blond hair and white eyelashes standing casually over her. It was Rol Swenson, the boy she had met in the cafeteria the day before.

"I said, buzz off. She's a friend of Doyle's."

"Oh, sorry. I didn't know."

Like magic Ginger was released and stood weak-kneed looking from one boy's face to the other. Her captor had been a fat kid with a mouthful of braces. "Thanks," she managed to say to Rol.

The other boy shrugged. "Give me a break," he said nervously. "How was I supposed to know?"

What does Doylita have to do with it? Ginger wondered. She left the boys arguing and ran back for her books. Then she headed up the steps and stood for several minutes watching what had become a frenzy on the lawn, worse than the day before.

Finally, Rol Swenson bounded up the steps toward Ginger. He stood over six feet tall, undoubtedly too mature to play such silly games. Ginger's heart flopped over as he pulled open the door and smiled at her. The blue shirt he wore matched the sparkling color of his eyes. Ginger's face flushed as she followed him into the front hall.

Just then Mr. Wintermeyer, the principal, stormed out of his office and rushed past. "What's going on!" he demanded and charged down the stairs.

Ginger watched him, wondering if her dad had called, then started up the steps to her locker. The blue shirt was no longer in sight. He saved my life, she thought, glowing inside. Who needs Lance Woodward?

She walked along the tiled hallway checking the locker numbers, then stopped next to 278. The door didn't look quite as chipped as it had the day before. Kids lined the hallway, banging open their lockers.

"Hi, Ginger." Corine glided down the hall with three other girls, all wearing pompons.

Ginger sighed and pulled out her notebook where she had written the combination to the lock.

When would Doylita show up? she wondered, looking down the hall past the row of noisy kids.

She turned to her locker and twirled the knob to the right, then the left, then right again. Yank! The metal stayed firm in its place. She looked down the hall again. No Doylita.

"Hi," Ginger said casually as a couple more shoe pompons went by. The yarn balls were beginning to look like some kind of club insignia.

She tried the lock again, making sure each time that the arrow rested precisely on the right notch.

"Having trouble there?" Lance Woodward grinned at her and leaned against the locker next to Ginger's, his books resting on his hip.

"What would you care? I could have been drowned out there."

"You aren't even wet. I tried to help you, remember?"

"I didn't need you then," Ginger said, concentrating again on her lock.

"Ah-ha! So you're admitting that you . . . perhaps . . . might have needed me later?"

"I'm going to be ill." Ginger twirled the knob to the last number and gave the lock a jerk. It should have opened, but it didn't. "I can't do anything right with you watching me!" She turned her back to Lance.

He leaned over her shoulder until she felt his breath on her ear.

"Didn't you learn anything yesterday in homeroom?" she asked.

Ginger pulled frantically at the lock several times, then knocked it against the locker door as hard as she could while Lance threw his head back and laughed.

"There's something wrong with this stupid thing!" she said and reached down to pick up her stack of books. "Why do they have to make these things so complicated anyway? You need a safecracker to open them!"

"What's your combination? I'll open it for you." Lance looked at her in a way that was almost nice.

"No way! I'm not telling you anything. I wouldn't trust anyone who would turn homeroom into a *gas chamber*!" And Ginger smiled, because she'd finally gotten the last word. Then she rushed away, not too sure where she was going—just away.

"Hay, wait a minute!" Lance called after her. "I'm a changed man. Give me a chance."

Ginger had walked only a short distance down the hall when she saw Doylita gluing pictures into someone else's locker. Why would she do that? Ginger wondered, but when she reached Doylita, she noticed the number 287 on the open locker door and all the familiar scratches.

With a sick feeling in the bottom of her stomach, the

facts dawned on her: she had been trying to open the wrong locker.

How could I be so stupid? Her face burned as she looked back to see if Lance was watching.

8.

"I'm not going to tell anyone," Lance promised in homeroom. But Ginger still did not trust him.

"It could have happened to anyone," she said. "Two eighty-seven and two seventy-eight are practically the same."

She looked up at Mr. Clarke, hoping he hadn't overheard this ridiculous conversation.

The teacher was printing an announcement on the board: *Pep assembly this a.m. Homeroom shortened to ten minutes.*

Doylita hadn't come in from the locker yet. Ginger looked anxiously toward the doorway. Where was the auditorium?

She was about to ask someone to go to the assembly with her when the sound of breaking glass brought the class to attention. Ginger whirled around on her stool, certain that Lance was in trouble again, but this time it was a girl in a striped shirt. Tiny bits of glass speckled the counter top in front of her.

"Beakers are a dollar apiece, Miss Warneke," Mr. Clarke barked. "You may break as many as you like. I'll just put them on your bill; you can pay me before the end of the quarter."

Bills? Ginger had heard nothing about bills.

"But it was an accident." The girl's face was scarlet.

"That's what they all say." Mr. Clarke smiled in a sinister way. "Woodward owes me two-fifty for the gas he used yesterday." He handed a green metal wastebasket to Ginger, who passed it back. Hunks of oddly shaped broken glass and coils of tubing covered the bottom. Ginger squinted at the number of "accidents" in disbelief. He must be getting rich, she thought.

The classroom rumbled with talk about Mr. Clarke and his bills until the bell sounded. Ginger checked the clock. What could have happened to Doylita? She had been at the locker only a few minutes before homeroom.

Kids rushed toward the doors. Lance pressed in behind Ginger. "You don't know where the auditorium is, right?"

Ginger refused to speak. Why should she give Lance the satisfaction of an answer, truthful or not? Besides, he was getting to be a real pain, showing up everywhere like a little brother.

Once out in the hallway, Ginger was pushed along with the crowd. She couldn't have moved in the opposite direction even if she had wanted to. Lance hovered behind her, bumping into her shoulder every few seconds as if to remind her that he was still there.

"I'm not paying any two-fifty for gas," he grumbled into her ear. "I didn't use any more than a dime's worth."

"You could have asphyxiated the whole class," Ginger said, "and that's manslaughter."

"Very funny. I didn't even know what it was. I thought it was water or something."

Ginger inched down the stairs with the crowd and craned her neck to see over the heads in front of her.

Maybe she would spot Doylita. Surely Lance wasn't hoping to sit with her! In high school a girl could sit with a boy once and everyone would think they were going together. Her reputation could be ruined on her second day at Alcott.

Ginger moved with the throng of noisy kids through double doors into a very old blue-velvet auditorium. "See, I knew exactly where to go," she told Lance triumphantly.

Rows of worn blue seats folded down quickly as kids filled the empty spaces. Faded velvet curtains hung heavily at opposite sides of a rounded stage.

Ginger scanned the seats for someone she recognized or for a single space where she could slip in without Lance.

"Hey, Woodward," someone called, "over here."

Lance brushed past. "See you later," he said to Ginger and crawled over a row of kids to sit next to a boy in a red sweat shirt.

Ginger watched him drop into his seat without giving her another glance. How do you like that? she thought indignantly. He had made her nervous for nothing!

She moved to the back of the auditorium, where extra chairs had been set up in every possible space. Shelley Franklin sat there, playing with the thick braid that hung over her shoulder. Saucers of light glinted off her glasses.

Ginger rushed toward her. "Hi. Can I sit with you?"

"Sure." Shelley patted the seat next to her.

Ginger settled happily on the aisle chair and looked toward the stage where a row of boys sat peering through the lights at the audience. "I don't care all that much about football. Too bad this isn't a talent show or a school play."

"Yeah," Shelley agreed.

Near the end of the row, leaning with his elbows on his knees, sat Rol Swenson!

"Hey, I know that guy!" Ginger exclaimed. "He saved me from the fountain this morning."

Ginger shifted to see around the kids sitting in front of her. "The third one from the end. He's wearing a blue shirt."

"Oh, yeah, I see him." Shelley twisted her braid. "Gee, he's really . . . unusual looking."

"The word is *fascinating*." Ginger could hardly contain her excitement. "I wonder why he's on stage. Maybe he's getting an award or something."

"He looks more weird than fascinating," Shelley commented.

A moment later Mr. Wintermeyer strode across the stage to the microphone and tapped it. The sound cracked through the auditorium, and all heads faced forward. The boys on stage looked toward the new principal.

"Before we begin, I have an announcement. The fountain outside your school is not a swimming pool. Its purpose is to beautify the school grounds. If you cannot refrain from misusing it, the fountain will have to be turned off . . . permanently. We've had parents calling the school this morning, and this has got to stop."

Parents, plural? Then someone other than her own father must have called. Ginger smiled at Shelley. "Hooray," she whispered.

". . . And I know none of you wants the fountain turned off."

"Yes, we do." Ginger leaned close to Shelley, and the two laughed together.

"Turn it off!" Shelley chanted, stomping her feet.

"Turn it off! Turn it off! Turn it off!" Ginger bravely took the lead, and within seconds a female chorus of jeering filled the auditorium, followed by boys screaming, "Leave it on!"

"Turn it off! Turn it off!" Ginger laughed uncontrollably. "Look what you've started," she hollered over the noise to Shelley.

"I know. Isn't it great?"

Mr. Wintermeyer paced across the stage as if he didn't know what to do. Finally he whacked the head of the microphone with a pen, sending an electric screech through the auditorium. Ginger plugged her ears.

"Now," he said, ignoring the protest. "I give you the Alcott football team." He gestured with a sweep of his hand for the row of boys to stand up.

At the same moment a band started playing somewhere out in the hall, and the auditorium doors flew wide open. Cheerleaders raced in and up onto the stage waving giant pompons. Ginger recognized Corine among them and three other girls who had been in Freman's with them the night before. Doylita's friends were all cheerleaders!

Drums and trumpets vibrated in Ginger's ears as the band came strutting down the aisle. They marched so close to her that she could have reached out and touched them.

The band paraded up the aisle and onto the stage, where the cheerleaders twirled in their short green skirts. On their shoes they all wore the smaller pompons from Freman's.

A small pang of jealousy seized Ginger. She could be wearing shoe poms, too, if only she'd had three dollars the day before.

Suddenly a hush washed over the auditorium as if

something were about to happen. Then the football players started to clap as out popped a little girl in a short skirt with black fur around the edges. She wore high, fur-trimmed boots and a hood with ears.

"Your Alcott Cougar!" Mr. Wintermeyer yelled into the microphone. The students cheered. Caught up in the excitement, Ginger yelled, too.

The girl turned around, stomping her feet and wiggling her hips. Long blond hair swung across her back.

Ginger stared at the familiar figure. "Oh, my gosh! It's Doylita!"

9.

"Do you know her?" Shelley asked in amazement.

"She's my locker partner," Ginger answered as casually as she could, then sank back in a trance to watch Doylita perform in front of the entire school. The girl gyrated to the music, kicking her feet high above her head and flinging her arms every which way, as if the rhythmic movements were more natural to her than walking. Her hair switched back and forth in a gold blur.

"She's really good," Shelley commented.

"I know." Why didn't she tell me? Ginger wondered. She thought back to the conversations they'd had the day before. Doylita had said that she'd been in the school a lot, but she hadn't said why.

The band music blared in a loud finale while Doylita flipped over backward and came down in a split. She waved her arms over her head as if the trick were no strain at all.

Then a short, muscular-looking man with bushy blond eyebrows jogged out onto the stage, and Mr. Wintermeyer introduced Jesse Willard, the football coach.

Jesse Willard . . . Doylita Willard. Could he be the father everyone was talking about? Suddenly Ginger understood. "Your dad will love the pompons," Corine had said. Doylita knew all the older boys and the cheerleaders. She probably lived out on the football field when she wasn't home or in school. No wonder Doylita knew her way around!

Mr. Willard introduced the players one by one. Ginger watched breathlessly as Rol Swenson stood up. Any friend of Doylita's was a friend of his, he had said.

What a day! Ginger thought. Imagine the luck; she was sharing a locker with one of the most important girls in the school.

The assembly ended with a reminder to attend the football game after school on Friday.

"Are you going?" Shelley asked.

"I guess so, as long as I'm stuck here."

"I suppose I am, too."

When Doylita bounced into English late, all eyes followed her to her seat, where she opened her book, flipped her hair back, and smiled on one side of her mouth.

She leaned toward Ginger. "Hi. You going downtown tonight?" The boy in front of them turned around and stared at Ginger as if he couldn't believe she knew the school mascot.

Goose bumps crawled over her. "Well . . . I . . .

sure, I guess so," she answered uncomfortably. "I didn't know you were the school mascot. Why didn't you tell me?"

"I thought everyone knew."

Later at the locker, Ginger looked in with dismay. "Gee, I see why you wanted the space to yourself. There's hardly any room for your outfit and boots. Do you want me to move out?" she offered, hoping Doylita would say no.

"That's okay. You're here now," Doylita answered.

"How did you get to be the Alcott cougar? Did you have to try out?"

Doylita jammed her costume into the locker on top of all the small items she had collected in the bottom. "My mom took off when I was five, and my dad didn't know what to do with me so he took me to football practices. You can figure out the rest. Anyway, I've been mascot for a long time," she explained proudly.

"I'm sorry about your mom," Ginger said.

"Why? I'm not. I do pretty much what I want."

What would it be like, Ginger wondered, to be on her own? Her parents tried to control everything she did. "Do you do all the housework?"

"Just about," Doylita answered, "but I think we're getting a dishwasher for Christmas. Last summer we redecorated the kitchen, and now we have a perfect spot for a dishwasher."

Ginger imagined choosing curtains for the kitchen. Doylita probably stayed out as late as she wanted, too, and bought her own clothes.

"Gee, that's great," Ginger said. "You're so lucky."

Doylita stepped up to reach the top shelf of the locker.

"My dad and I get along fine," she went on. "He doesn't bother me, and I don't bother him."

Maybe it would be fun to be short and not have a mother, Ginger thought. Neither seemed to bother Doylita. And being the school mascot must be exciting; she was popular without even trying.

Ginger traded her English book for algebra and closed the locker.

The two walked on. Ginger noticed heads turning to look at Doylita.

"Hi, Doyle. How's it goin'?"

"Hey, John. Not too shabby. Are you ready for the game?"

"I'll be ready Friday afternoon." John was one of the football players, but he looked more fat than muscular.

Doylita grinned in her usual lopsided way. "Hi, Rol."

Ginger jerked to attention as Rol Swenson approached.

"We're going to be awesome this year," he said, draping an arm around John's shoulder. "No more ten-and-nothing seasons for us, right?" He glanced briefly down at Doylita, then smiled at Ginger, whose chest turned suddenly tight.

The boys talked for several minutes, but Ginger was too unnerved to hear anything they said.

Finally Doylita's voice cut in. "See you later, guys."

Ginger's eyes followed Rol down the hall.

"You've got a crush on Rol-and," Doylita crooned.

"I do not," Ginger insisted quickly. "I've never liked a boy in my life."

"Okay, but I think he likes *you*."

"How do you know?" She swallowed and tried to look casual, as if she really didn't care.

"I just know. Besides, he asked me if you were going to the party Friday night."

"What party?"

"We have parties at my house after the games. It's mainly for the cheerleaders and the team, but you can come, too, if you want to."

Ginger's stomach rolled over. She'd never been to a party with boys before. "I don't know." It sounded fun, yet scary at the same time. "What kinds of things do you do?"

Doylita sighed with annoyance. "Eat hot dogs and dance. You don't have to come if you don't want to."

"It's not that I don't want to, it's just that . . . well, I don't know what my parents will say."

One hand went to Doylita's hip. "For heaven's sake, you're in high school. Your *parents* aren't invited. Besides, Rol will really be disappointed if you don't show up."

"Are you sure, Doylita? Did he really say that?"

"Would I lie?"

Ginger looked down at her and considered the possibility. Rol *had* saved her from getting drenched in the fountain, and he *had* smiled at her.

"I'll tell you what," Doylita bargained. "You can sit with me on the player's bench during the game. Then we can take off for my house to get things set up."

The player's bench? Where everyone would see her? She'd feel like a fool with nothing official to do there.

"Are you sure it's okay?"

"Of course it's okay. My dad doesn't care what I do."

"That would be fun . . . I guess," Ginger said.

10.

During lunch Ginger sat in the same tiny space she had occupied the day before, wedged between Doylita and Rol Swenson. The cheerleaders, still wearing their green skirts and sweaters, all sat at the same table, too. Doylita introduced them to Ginger. The black girl across the table was Mindy. Next to her sat Chris, the blond who had been with them in Freman's, then Janet and Kim, who almost looked like twins with their short brown hair worn the same way. Corine sat directly opposite Rol.

Ginger wiggled nervously, trying not to touch Rol's arm with her own, but he seemed almost to be leaning on her.

I must be imagining this, she thought. In spite of what Doylita had said, she couldn't believe that he liked her. But the thought that he might be leaning toward her on purpose pleased her, in a scary kind of way.

Ginger examined her right arm, hanging loosely from her shoulder, and looked up at Rol, who was definitely sitting at a tilt.

She reached carefully for a carrot stick and bit the end off as quietly as she could, then chewed once or twice and swallowed. This is miserable, she thought. How could people ever stand to be married?

"I really blew it this morning," Corine said. "I completely forgot that second cheer. We'd better have another practice soon."

"I thought you were good," Ginger told her. "I didn't notice anything wrong."

Rol looked down at Ginger. "She always says that. Then she waits for someone to tell her how great she is."

"I do not!" Corine sailed her straw at Rol, who laughed and ducked, rubbing his head on Ginger's arm.

Ginger looked down at the white-blond hair nestled against her elbow and wondered what to do. Her face burned as she drew away.

" 'Scuse me," Rol said.

Doylita giggled.

There was silence around the table. Corine looked from Rol to Ginger and back again.

"I'm stuffed." Ginger coughed. "See you later, Doylita."

"Wait a minute. What's the hurry?"

Ginger tried not to look at Rol, whose eyes were fixed on her face. "Nothing." No one believed her, she knew, but Ginger could not sit another minute next to *him*. She felt as if a bomb were about to go off in her brain.

"Well, I'm not done eating." Doylita complained. "Go ahead. I'll see you after fourth period."

Ginger rushed out into the hall, where she could be alone and think over the confusion she felt. If it were true that Rol liked her, what should she do about it? If she admitted that she liked him, too, something would be expected to happen: phone calls, walking together between classes, going out on dates. What had she gotten herself into now? Maybe he thought she was older.

Ginger entered the art room. Smells of oil paints, linseed oil and gum erasers greeted her, bringing a sense of safety and happiness. She tacked a fresh piece of charcoal paper to a board and placed it on an easel. By the end of the class period something new from her own mind would exist in this empty white space. The process always amazed and excited her.

All through art class Ginger alternated between goose bumps and a queasy stomach. She stared dazedly toward the front of the room, not really seeing the apples and oranges that the teacher had arranged in a bowl for the class to sketch. She drew a line, then erased, drew a second line and erased again. Nothing seemed to penetrate the buzzing confusion in her mind.

Finally, her pencil created a masculine face with pale, blank-looking eyes that stared out of the paper at her; not exactly the assignment, but she hoped the portrait would do.

Drawing always had a miraculous, soothing effect on her, and by the time art was over, Ginger felt ready to concentrate on Mr. Clarke's class.

"Science is my best subject," sighed a girl with full pink lips. "If I get bored, I can just stare at *him*."

Halfway through class Ginger noticed that the back of the girl's hair was wet. She tapped her on the shoulder. "Did you get thrown into the fountain?"

Without taking her eyes off Mr. Clarke, the girl leaned back and said, "No, I had P.E. last period. We started taking showers today."

Ginger straightened. "You're kidding!"

Mr. Clarke stopped pacing abruptly. "No, Miss Wilson, I'm not kidding. Amoebae really do multiply by dividing."

Ginger dropped her head onto her hand. The pale green classroom and her countertop all seemed to spin around her head. Life had gone crazy in the last few days. How was she going to live through it all? There were so many things to worry about, except that there was no time to worry. For the next hour she was supposed to think about amoebas.

"Pay attention, please!" Mr. Clarke barked at her. "Everything I'm telling you will be on a quiz Monday."

When the bell rang, ending fifth period, Ginger had no choice but to head for the gym. This is stupid, she thought angrily. I take showers at home. Why do I have to take them at school, too?

Doylita danced into the gym behind the P.E. teacher, crossing her eyes and making faces at her. She looked like a seven-year-old as she made her way to the bench where Ginger and Shelley were sitting.

"Don't you like Miss Stanley?" Ginger asked.

"She's a slut."

"A what?" The teacher was tall, with an almost-pretty face and brown hair held in a ponytail at the nape of her neck.

"Trust me. I know her."

Ginger exchanged glances with Shelley. What was *that* all about? she wondered. "I heard we have to take showers today," she said, changing the subject.

"It's state law."

"It's the law? Why?"

"Because . . . it just is." Doylita bent over and re-tied one of her green-and-yellow shoe poms. "It's no big deal. You just get a few drops of water on your back and they think you've had a shower."

"But we have to take all our clothes off, don't we?"

Doylita pulled her mouth into a half-smile. "Well, of course."

After playing basketball for what seemed like a very

56

short time, the class lined up in front of the locker room door. Shelley breathed heavily behind Ginger.

"Hey, you're good," Shelley said. "Are you going to try out for the girls' team?"

"I don't know," Ginger answered. "Are you?"

"I'm thinking about it. The problem is getting home so late. At Fairview I could have walked."

"I have a couple of announcements," Miss Stanley said.

Here it comes, Ginger thought. Showers.

"Monday each of you is to have your regulation gym outfit: green shorts, white shirt, cotton socks, and sneakers. No hard-soled shoes. We're late getting started this year because of the transfers, so you'll be marked down if you aren't prepared to dress out on Monday. Any questions?"

Ginger looked at Doylita. The gym buzzed with whispers.

Miss Stanley held up her hand for attention. "Also," she continued, "this is the time, during puberty, when perspiration glands become active. . . ."

You can say that again, Ginger said to herself.

". . . so you'll be taking showers in high school." With no further explanation she turned and made a forward gesture with her arm. "Follow me."

"What she means," Doylita broadcast in a sarcastic voice, "is that when you're a teen-ager you start to *sweat*. We're not in a doctor's office, you know." One big snicker issued from the class.

Ginger managed a weak laugh and peered over the heads in front of her as the freshman girls filed into the locker room.

Cracked concrete floors edged with gray lockers and wooden benches extended the full length of the room to a wall of stained mirrors.

"Where are the showers?" one voice asked.

The class moved past a cage where a girl handed each person a bumpy white towel.

"Gee, it's so small," Ginger complained as she unfolded hers.

"You sure this isn't a dishcloth?" Shelley asked.

"I think teachers should shower, too," Doylita announced in a loud voice. "They sweat as much as we do."

"Doylita!" Ginger nudged her. What did she have against Miss Stanley?

The teacher glanced at Doylita but didn't say anything, then led the class through the locker room and around the corner where steam poured out of a wide doorway. Half a dozen shower heads spewed hot water into one large drain in the middle of the floor.

Ginger gasped. "You mean, we have to shower *together*?"

"When you're through, give your name to the attendant and she'll check you off." With that, Miss Stanley disappeared, leaving thirty girls to look at each other and wonder who would go first.

"I can't take showers," one girl said. "I have an infected toe."

"I'm having my period," someone else reported, and about half the class said that they were having their periods, too. The other half didn't seem to care at all and started to undress in front of everyone. Doylita was among them.

Ginger swallowed. It would be best to get it over with quickly, she decided. Shelley seemed to come to the same conclusion as she removed her shoes and socks and arranged them neatly on the bench behind her.

Ginger wriggled out of her clothes, carefully holding her towel in front of her, then ran for the shower. As the warm water sprinkled down on her, washing away the sweat, she realized her second day at Alcott had begun and ended in the same way; with water. First, she had narrowly escaped a dunking in the fountain, and now she was standing naked with a bunch of girls she hardly knew, taking a shower.

Being careful not to wash away the make-up she had so carefully applied that morning, Ginger held up her long hair and rinsed the perspiration from her neck. Then she rubbed at her arms, gave her name to the attendant who sat on a stool just outside the shower, and started to dry off.

Unexpectedly, the sound of the school bell pierced the moist air. Ginger looked up. Girls rushed madly in all directions.

"Oh, my gosh!" one girl screamed. "I've got to catch a bus!" and she left the gym without tying her shoes.

The attendance girl reached in and turned off the water. Suddenly all was silent except for a few drips.

"Hurry up!" Doylita said. She leaned against the wall with her book bag hugged in her arms. "I want to beat the crowd to Freman's and see about a gym outfit."

Ginger buttoned her blouse and looked at Doylita. She did mean *buy* a gym outfit, didn't she?

11

The girls merged with the crowd outside the school and made their way downtown. At least Ginger didn't have to worry about the fountain when she walked with Doylita. Taking the city bus was the perfect solution; by the time it stopped at the school, she was safely aboard.

Reaching Freman's in one big mob, the crowd spread out like a spilled bag of jelly beans, finding their way into every aisle. Doylita and Ginger took the escalator straight to the girl's department.

Mannequins stood on raised areas throughout the store in bright, fall clothes. Ginger loved the new outfits in oranges, browns, and golds. A feeling of exhilaration surged through her at the thought of the brisk days to come, with leaves falling and the wind blowing.

Doylita did not seem to notice the new displays. She moved quickly to the gym outfits stacked neatly on a table, then rummaged through them until she found her size, leaving a pile of unfolded blouses and shorts.

Without thinking Ginger began folding them up again.

"What are you doing?" Doylita stared at Ginger's hands. "They hire women to straighten these things. That's what they do all day long . . . straighten things. If no one messed anything up, they wouldn't have jobs." She talked as if Ginger should have known better.

"May I help you?" A saleslady flashed a stiff smile and looked the girls over as if she suspected something.

Ginger dropped the blouse she'd been folding and stepped away from the table. She glanced at Doylita.

"No, thank you. We're just browsing," Doylita said calmly.

The woman hesitated, then walked off.

Ginger picked up a pair of shorts and checked the price tag. "Gee, they're expensive. Is that for the whole outfit, or just the shorts?"

"Just the shorts, of course," Doylita said in her usual know-it-all voice. "Come on, let's try these on."

"I'm not getting mine today," Ginger hedged. "I'll probably come down Saturday."

"I just want to see what size I wear."

Doylita led the way through a curtain to a long row of fitting rooms and went into a cubicle on the end. Ginger followed. Feet and piles of clóthes were visible under some of the other doors.

Doylita took off her jeans and put on the green shorts.

"They fit perfectly," Ginger said, looking down at the small figure in the mirror. She leaned awkwardly against the back wall as a nervous feeling came over her.

Doylita pulled at the waistband and looked at herself in the mirror, then took the pins out of the blouse and tried it on, too. The sleeves were a little big, but four was the smallest size they had.

Ginger stood watching, shifting her weight from one foot to the other. "They look fine," she said. "Let's go."

Doylita took off the blouse and dropped it on the floor, then pulled her jeans on over the shorts.

I knew it! Ginger thought. What nerve! "Doylita! You can't do that!"

Innocent blue eyes looked up. Doylita sighed with annoyance. "It's no big deal. The stores expect you to take things. Why do you think they have insurance?" she fastened her jeans.

Ginger looked at the floor, feeling sick inside. What was she supposed to do now?

"If you want to pay that much for one lousy pair of shorts, go ahead," Doylita went on. "I wouldn't mind paying for things if the prices weren't so high. It's the store's own fault."

"But that's not fair!" Ginger said. "You're getting a free gym outfit, while everyone else has to buy one!"

Doylita shrugged as if she didn't care. She refolded the blouse and slipped it into her book bag, then bounced out of the fitting room.

She knows I'm not going to tell, Ginger thought angrily, not when she's the school mascot and the daughter of the football coach. Who would believe me?

As the girls left, Doylita picked up a pair of white socks and went to the cash register to pay for them.

"Why did you do that?" Ginger asked, as they stopped to look again at the shoe pom display. The green-and-yellow pompons had been restocked.

"I don't want them to get suspicious. If you pay for something, it makes you a regular customer."

She really thinks it's okay! Ginger thought. "Brother, what they don't know."

"Hey, listen here." Doylita wheeled around, the sweet, innocent look gone from her eyes. "Everyone takes things once in a while, so don't go acting like some kind of saint."

Ginger cast her eyes to the floor. Not everyone, she wanted to say, and she thought of Paula and her brother and, most of all, a boy like Rol Swenson.

Doylita replaced her smile and pulled four pompons off the cardboard shoe, tossing them into the air and juggling them as if she were doing a circus act.

Ginger watched for a minute, then reached into the circle and grabbed a pompon. Doylita caught another one, but the remaining two fell to the floor.

"Hey, you spoiled my rhythm. What'd you do that for?"

Inside, Ginger laughed a little at her private protest. "I couldn't resist."

Doylita bent down to pick up the pompons, then stood up and glared at Ginger.

"Where in the world have you been this time?" Mrs. Wilson hollered at Ginger when she finally got home at five-thirty. "I told you Mark has a soccer game tonight and I have a meeting."

"I went downtown with Doylita. I thought you said I could—"

"I never expected you to be *this* late," her mother said. She threw a jacket over her arm and called to Mark.

Ginger slid her hand along the banister as she ran up the stairs. "I'll try to be earlier tomorrow, I promise."

"Mark, get down here this minute. We're going to be late." Mrs. Wilson appeared at the foot of the stairs and stretched to look up at Ginger. "I don't know. It seems to me staying downtown this late every night is a good way to get into trouble."

"I'm not going to get into any trouble," Ginger offered weakly. In her mind she saw the green shorts under Doylita's jeans.

Mark sat in the middle of the hallway tying his spiked soccer shoes. He smiled as Ginger passed him.

"What's so funny?" Ginger demanded and stepped on her brother's foot.

"Ow! What'd I do to you?"

A huge sigh came from the living room below, and

Mrs. Wilson raced up the stairs, her car keys jingling. "What's going on?" she yelled, mostly at Ginger. "Can't you kids see I'm in a hurry? I've got to get to this soccer game, then to the grocery store, then—"

"She stepped on my foot . . . on purpose."

"You had it coming," Ginger grumbled.

Mom stood between them. "What's the matter with you tonight, Ginger? What did he do to you?"

"He smiled," she said simply, knowing how stupid it sounded.

Mrs. Wilson's eyebrow arched. "That's *it*?"

Suddenly Ginger's mood plummeted. "O-oh! No one ever listens to me around here. I have enough problems at school without this." She ran into her room and slammed the door as hard as she could, knocking her bathrobe, nightgown, a pair of jeans, and a belt off the doorknob.

"And don't slam the door," her mother yelled after her.

Ginger could feel Mark smiling, even though she couldn't see him. Doylita had it made, she thought, with no mother or brother to interfere in her life.

A few minutes later, with the house to herself, Ginger went into Mark's room to get his stuffed bear. She yanked its clothes off—some little pajamas her mother had made —and set it on the ledge outside of Mark's window.

Let him look for it till Christmas, she thought. He'll never find it. Maybe the weather will turn cold and the stupid thing will freeze to death. She smiled, feeling mean inside, and bounced downstairs for a snack.

Ginger dropped a Pop Tart into the toaster and sat down at the kitchen table with her book bag. As she reached in for her math book, she felt two soft yarn balls.

12.

Where in the world did these come from? Ginger wondered. Then her forehead tingled as the scene reeled back through her mind; Doylita had juggled the pompons, dropped two of them on the floor, and bent down to pick them up. Had she put them back on the cardboard shoe? Ginger couldn't remember. Maybe she had dropped them into Ginger's book bag.

She gulped and held the yarn balls against her cheeks, feeling their softness. I can't keep them, she thought, but she bent over her shoes and set the pompons in place as if they belonged to her. She stood up and walked carefully across the floor looking down at her feet. One pompon fell off and she picked it up. It wouldn't hurt to tie them into her shoelaces, she decided.

A moment later, Ginger was twirling around the kitchen, wiggling her hips and stomping her feet. She kicked one leg high into the air and felt a little thrill as she watched the pompons bounce on the toes of her shoes. Then she sat down at the kitchen table again and stared down at her feet. Too bad she hadn't had the three dollars to buy them herself.

Suddenly the door leading from the garage opened, and Ginger's father stood in the doorway with his briefcase.

"Hi," he said cheerfully. "Don't look so scared. It's only me. I live here, remember?"

"Hi." Ginger held her hand over her chest to quiet her beating heart. She tucked her feet under her chair.

Mr. Wilson looked down. "Are those the pompons you wanted so badly?"

"Uh . . . yeah."

"How'd you come up with the money?"

"I didn't," Ginger answered. "A girl gave me these." She cringed. Why had she lied? "I'll probably give them back, though, or pay for them." She managed to smile, congratulating herself on her quick thinking.

"You can't do that," Mr. Wilson said. "You'll hurt the girl's feelings." He took a second look at her shoes as he opened his briefcase on the kitchen counter. "They're nothing but yarn. You could have made a pair for fifty cents."

"I know." Ginger laughed nervously. Actually, she hadn't thought of that.

Her father left the kitchen and Ginger let out a sigh of relief, but the feeling only lasted a second. If she told the truth now, she would have to admit that she had lied in the first place. And there had been no reason to protect Doylita. Ginger could have told her father that her locker partner had stolen the pompons and passed them off on her.

She slid her chair out and bent over her shoes once more. She knew what was right, but the rules never seemed to apply to Doylita, so why should they apply to her? Life was not fair. But sometimes you could think about something too much. The shoe poms were only little balls of yarn after all. How important could they really be?

Ginger spent the next two hours trying to call Paula from the upstairs phone. She hadn't talked to her since she'd changed schools. Life had changed so much in such a short time, and there had been no one to tell. "Where *is* she?" Ginger complained as she banged down the receiver.

A second later the phone rang. Paula! Ginger thought. "Hell-o."

"I've called every Wilson in the book," Doylita's voice chirped.

"Hi," Ginger said blandly and looked down at her shoes where the bright yarn balls were still tied.

"What did your parents say about Friday? You can go, can't you?"

"I don't know," Ginger told her. "My mom just got home."

"Then go ask. I'll wait."

The pompons, Ginger thought. I've got to find out where they came from. Instead, she said, "Hold on. I'll be right back."

Ginger descended the stairs slowly. Actually, she wasn't so sure she wanted to go to the party. What if Rol didn't really like her? Worse yet, what if he did? How could she talk to a senior?

They'll never let me go, Ginger concluded confidently as she approached the kitchen. She could tell Doylita she wasn't allowed to go to boy-girl parties, and it would probably be true. After all, she wasn't even fifteen yet.

"Um . . ." Ginger's breath caught in her throat. "Doylita's on the phone. She wants to know if I can go with her to the football game Friday and then to a party at her house . . . with boys." Ginger stood playing with the collar on her shirt.

"You don't even like football, do you?" her father asked.

"Well, I've never actually seen a whole game."

"We'll have to know the details," he said. "How will you get to the party? Who will bring you home?"

"There won't be any alcohol or drugs, will there?" her mother wanted to know.

"I don't think so," Ginger said. "The party is at the coach's house near the school. But, I suppose I could come home right after the game."

"You don't sound very enthusiastic," her mother commented. "Do you really want to go?"

"Of course I want to go," Ginger argued. What am I saying? she wondered.

"Of course she does," her father echoed. "She's in high school now."

Mrs. Wilson looked worried, as if she were on the verge of saying no.

"Please," Ginger heard herself plead. It must be a habit, she thought, instinctively trying to talk them into giving permission.

Finally her dad said, "The party sounds okay as long as it's at the coach's house. You can call me when it's over if you need a ride." He smiled as if he were doing her a favor.

"Thanks," Ginger said uncertainly and went back upstairs to the telephone.

"I can go," she said to Doylita. The one time she had counted on her parents to say no, they had said yes. And it was her own fault.

Doylita squealed, "That's great! We can hurry downtown Friday after school to pick up the cake at the bakery, then we can leave it in the back of my dad's station wagon during the game."

. . .

Wednesday, after school, Doylita spent nearly an hour looking at gold-posted earrings. The saleslady's back had been turned toward the cash register, and Ginger felt sure Doylita would steal as many as she could get away with.

"I'm definitely getting my ears pierced," Doylita said. "Do you think I'd look best in silver . . . ?" She dangled an earring near her earlobe. "Or gold?"

"I don't know," Ginger said and edged away to look at watches in a glass case, expecting Doylita to make her move at any moment. If she had to walk downtown, at least she could stay away from Doylita while she was ripping things off.

But the next thing she knew, Doylita was standing at the cash register paying for two pairs of earrings: one silver and one gold.

Maybe I'm a good influence. Ginger smiled at the thought.

Thursday night Ginger stared at the ceiling in her bedroom until after two o'clock. The pompons were in her dresser drawer. She hadn't asked Doylita about them, nor had Doylita mentioned them. Maybe they weren't stolen after all. Ginger couldn't really believe this after the gym suit incident, but it did seem strange that she had never said anything about the pompons. And she *had* paid for the earrings.

Worrying about the party was keeping her awake, too. After tomorrow night, Rol would know how shy and stupid she really was. If he liked her now, he wouldn't then.

At a quarter to two, Ginger finally made her way in the dark to the kitchen where she made a piece of toast and poured herself a glass of juice. As she headed back to her room, the mantle clock in the living room struck two.

A chorus of voices, footsteps, and running water woke her in the morning. Her eyes burned as if she hadn't slept at all, which was practically true. She had counted on Friday never coming, but here it was.

Nervously she showered and put on the outfit she had finally chosen the night before, tied on her shoes, and went to her dresser. She pulled open the drawer slowly, carefully, as if she expected a coiled rattlesnake to strike out at her. Ginger reached in for the soft yarn balls.

A moment later she ventured down the stairs for breakfast.

"Why are you wearing that dumb green skirt?" Mark asked.

"Don't bug me," Ginger warned him.

"What now?" her mother asked.

"It's none of his business what I wear."

Mrs. Wilson looked over Ginger's outfit. "Why are you wearing *that*? I ironed yesterday. Didn't you see all those clean clothes in your closet?"

"What's wrong with my old green skirt? I like it."

"It's getting kind of short, don't you think?"

Ginger pulled at the dark green corduroy and looked down at her knees. "Maybe . . . a little."

"She thinks she's a cheerleader," Mark put in. Several cornflakes flew out of his mouth as he spoke.

"Look at that! He's disgusting," Ginger complained. "I'd like to know why no one ever says anything to him about his manners. He acts however he wants and no one even cares."

"That's enough, Ginger. Mark, have some manners."

Mrs. Wilson looked again at her daughter's clothes. "Well, it's up to you, I guess. Will you have time to change before the party?"

Sometimes Ginger wanted to scream when her mother asked so many questions. "This *is* what I'm wearing to the party," she explained. "I don't want to be the only one not dressed in school colors."

"See, I told you," Mark mumbled through a full mouth. "She's even wearing those things on her shoes."

Ginger looked down at her feet. "They're not things; they're pompons." The decision had come to her sometime during the night. She honestly did not know where the pompons had come from, so if anyone asked about them, she could tell the truth.

"You look fine, Ginger," her mother finally decided. "You'd better hurry, now. Here's your lunch money." She kissed Ginger on the cheek. "Have a good time after school. Don't forget to call when it's over. My goodness," she added, "you're as tall as I am. I guess you really are growing up."

Ginger forced a smile and said good-bye. She sure didn't feel very grown-up. What teen-ager would rather stay home where it was safe than go to a party?

13.

All day Ginger tugged at her skirt. Doylita looked down at the shoe poms several times but didn't say anything.

"I like your green outfit," Corine said at lunchtime. "You almost look like a cheerleader."

"Really? I was afraid I looked silly. The thing is, my mom forgot to iron and I had to wear this old skirt," Ginger lied. "I've had it since fifth grade."

"What a lucky coincidence." Corine exchanged glances with the girl across the table, and they smiled at each other.

"Yeah . . . I guess it was." Were they making fun of her? Ginger looked down at her plate and pushed her lima beans to the side. She felt out of sync, like an old movie that ran a split second behind its sound track.

It wasn't until after school that her mood improved.

The entire student body seemed to explode through the doors at once, charged with excitement over the game. And this time Ginger would be part of the action. She hurried after Doylita, not wanting to miss a thing.

"Come on," Doylita called. "We barely have time to make it to the bakery before the game." She skipped backward a few feet ahead of Ginger.

Two blocks before they arrived at the bakery, warm doughy smells wafted through the air to tease Ginger's nose and trigger her appetite.

"Smells good," Ginger said. "I'm starved."

The girls opened the door and stepped into the bakery. A man standing at the counter pushed his hairy arms into the pockets of bib overalls and chatted with the clerk who crouched behind the glass cases.

Ginger and Doylita stood in the middle of the small shop waiting their turn and looked at the goodies on the shelves. Cream oozed out the ends of the chocolate eclairs onto a row of frosted pumpkin cookies. Cherry pies and apple fritters covered the bottom shelf.

On top of the counter stood a tall wedding cake with

pink roses curling from one layer to the next and some baskets of breadsticks. Ginger's stomach grumbled just looking at them. It would be hours before they got anything to eat at the party.

Near the far wall sat a wicker basket piled full of sugary little doughnut holes. Doylita moved over and stood near them.

Ginger's skin prickled as she watched Doylita's face change from innocent to sly. Except for the one man, they were the only customers in the store. The saleslady was behind the counter, reaching for pastries on the bottom shelf.

Doylita paid for the earrings, Ginger remembered. Maybe she'll pay for some doughnut holes, too.

Doylita's hand moved up and grabbed two or three of the sugary balls, then popped them into her mouth one by one.

Ginger look away.

"Take some," Doylita whispered. "They're just the holes out of the middle of the doughnuts. They're free. If we don't take them, they'll all be thrown out."

Then why are you being so sneaky? Ginger wanted to ask, but she already knew the answer: the doughnut holes weren't free at all.

Still, it didn't seem as bad as taking whole doughnuts or roses off the cake. They couldn't be worth much—unless you were practically starving to death, as Ginger was.

Doylita's eyes rolled toward the ceiling as if she couldn't believe anyone could be so dumb.

The man and the saleslady continued to talk while Doylita stuffed her mouth.

Ginger walked up to the counter and sniffed. Maybe she could try just one. If the lady said anything, she could tell her she thought they were free; that's what Doylita had told her, after all.

Ginger slid her fingers up to the basket and drummed them a few times while she caught her breath. Her jaws ached with hunger. She moved in closer and leaned on the glass as Doylita had done. The doughnut holes were only a few inches from her hand.

The saleslady reached for an eclair from behind the counter while the man in overalls looked on. Neither of them seemed to notice Ginger. It would be so incredibly easy to take a few, she thought.

Ginger looked nervously at Doylita, who mouthed the words, *go ahead*. Should she or shouldn't she? Once it would have been a simple decision. Stealing was wrong. Period. But now the choice was not so clear. She had seen her mother sample a grape once at the grocery store. There was no difference really between a grape and a doughnut hole. And why should Doylita get anything she wanted free, while Ginger always had to pay?

Ginger kept her eye on the saleslady as she reached into the basket. Her heart pounded wildly. The doughnut holes felt warm and softer than she expected, covered with a sticky glaze. Ginger grabbed three and stood frozen, her hand halfway between the basket and her chest.

"I guess that'll do it," the man with the hairy arms said as he took out his wallet.

Perspiration seemed to ooze suddenly from every pore of Ginger's body. The saleslady placed one last eclair into a box and stood up.

Panicked, Ginger dropped the doughnut holes back into the basket and pushed her sticky hand into the linty pocket of her corduroy skirt. Glaze stuck between her fingers and under her fingernails.

Doylita stood near the wedding cake, examining the plastic bride and groom, acting as if she had never seen Ginger before. Ginger pulled her hand out of her pocket and let her arm hang loosely at her side. She wiggled her fingers wishing she could lick them.

"May I help you?"

Ginger tried to swallow but choked instead and started to cough. Her face flushed so that her eyes seemed to bulge and her armpits went on like faucets.

"Um . . . (cough) . . . well, I. . . ."

"Are you all right?" the saleslady asked. "Here, let me get you a drink."

She handed a paper cup of lukewarm water to Ginger, who took a sip and breathed deeply a couple of times, then gave the cup back. Sugar from the doughnut holes glistened all over the blue-and-white-striped sides, but the woman didn't seem to notice.

"Thanks. I'm okay now." Why me? Ginger wondered. These things never seemed to happen to Doylita. She pushed her sticky hand back into her pocket.

Doylita stepped up. "She's just getting over a cold," she explained, smiling sweetly.

Another cough escaped from Ginger's throat.

Doylita handed the woman a piece of paper. "We're here to pick up that cake for Alcott High School."

"Oh, yes. Just a minute."

The instant the woman disappeared, Doylita doubled over in a fit of giggles. A queasy wave tumbled through Ginger's stomach. She had almost gotten caught stealing!

Doylita straightened abruptly when the saleslady returned with a long pink box, which she opened for the girls. Yellow icing covered an oblong cake with green lettering that spelled out, *Alcott Cougars.* Plastic players decorated the top.

"Ooh!" Doylita squealed. "Not too shabby."

All Ginger wanted to do was get out of the bakery before she exploded, but Doylita seemed determined to examine each of the little figures.

"This one's the quarterback." She nudged Ginger and pointed to a green plastic man. "Isn't he cute?"

"Doylita, let's get going." Ginger wiggled her fingers nervously inside her pocket. If the saleslady noticed the sugar on her hand, she was sunk.

Finally, Doylita closed the lid on the box and handed the woman a twenty-dollar bill. Ginger's eyes focused on the money. If Doylita had that much, why didn't she pay for the doughnut holes? She could have bought enough for both of them.

"Fourteen, fifteen, and twenty." The saleslady counted the change into Doylita's hand. Ginger edged toward the door. Slowly Doylita picked up the cake box as if nothing were unusual at all. The basket of doughnut holes was almost empty.

Ginger's nerves tightened like rubber bands. She could see the need to act casual, but Doylita seemed almost to be teasing the woman, daring her to catch them. She sauntered toward the door allowing her hair to swing across her back, wiggling her hips more than usual.

A few feet outside the bakery, Doylita broke into an awkward run, cake box and book bag bouncing along with her. Ginger followed, feeling the eyes of the saleswoman on her back all the way to the corner where they turned and were soon out of sight.

Doylita stopped and sank down in the shade of a big

maple tree, then threw her head back in hysterical laughter.

"Why did you run?" Ginger asked, out of breath. "Now she'll know who ate those doughnut holes. She probably thinks I took some, too."

"You almost did."

"I know." Ginger wiped her sticky hand on the grass. "I don't know what got into me. I was just so hungry . . . all those smells. I've never done anything like that before."

"Sure, you have."

"No, I haven't."

Doylita grinned and pointed to Ginger's shoes. "You're wearing the pompons, aren't you? I figured you would."

Ginger's face flushed. She had known the truth all along, but hearing the words sent a shock through her chest. "So you did steal them!"

"I didn't *steal* them," Doylita insisted. "I just sort of ripped them off. Like I told you before, the stores have insurance. They expect a few losses."

"I'm taking these things back to Freman's!" Ginger said suddenly and bent over to untie her shoes.

"You can't. They're used." Doylita was so calm that Ginger wanted to shake her.

"Well, I can't keep them, that's for sure."

Doylita's hand went to her forehead. "I don't believe this. Are you for real?" She sighed with annoyance. "Okay, I'll tell you what you can do: next time you're in Freman's, leave three dollars on the counter."

Ginger thought for a moment. Yes, she could do that. She retied her shoe. "Don't think for a minute that I won't." She stood up and started walking back to the school.

"Look," Doylita lectured as she followed along. "Everyone takes things once in a while. You act as though you just committed the crime of the century. Everyone rips things off."

"Not everyone," Ginger insisted. A clear picture of Rol Swenson bobbed up in her mind like the answer in a Magic Eight Ball.

14.

The band, in their green uniforms and gold braid, gathered near the fountain. The cheerleaders joined them, forming a line in front of the drummers. Doylita positioned herself in the lead. Ginger stood off to the side, awaiting Doylita's signal to march across to the football field.

Already kids swarmed over the bleachers, some with red-and-white banners or pompons, which meant the Jefferson bus had arrived. A row of five cheerleaders in red-fringed cowgirl outfits jumped around in front of the stands. Somewhere Paula was probably watching for Ginger.

Players from both teams practiced on the football field, but in their uniforms they all looked alike. Maybe from the bench she would be able to pick out Rol Swenson.

For the moment, the incident at the bakery was forgotten as Ginger joined in the excitement over Alcott's first game. Doylita's arm struck forward, and the band started playing "Fight, Alcott, Fight" with a rhythm that drummed in Ginger's ears. Her chest pounded as the group moved across the street.

Ginger half-walked, half-marched beside the cheerleaders, wondering how she could best fit in. At the same time she looked for Paula's face in the crowd.

The band marched up into the stands, and Ginger took her place alone on the bench while Doylita twisted and twirled out on the field. Ginger squirmed, wondering how many eyes were on her. If only she could sneak into the stands where no one would notice her.

When the game finally started, Doylita plunked down next to Ginger. Red and green helmets cracked together as one player after another was tackled and fell to the ground.

"Rol is number twelve," Doylita teased.

"Oh, is he?" Ginger scanned the field. Just as she spotted number twelve, he backed up to throw the ball but was tackled before he could release it.

Jesse Willard ran back and forth in front of the bench yelling at the players. "Get it together, Swenson!" he screamed. "Moseby, if you blow it like that one more time, I'm pulling you off the field."

Doylita smiled with pride. "Hey, Dad!" she called. The coach did not seem to hear her. "Dad!"

Coach Willard turned and scowled at Doylita. Ginger watched the smile slip off her face.

"What did you want to tell him?" Ginger asked.

"Nothing!" was Doylita's cold reply.

"If you guys need a nap, let me know," the coach continued. "Maybe we can reschedule the game."

At half time the band filed out onto the football field. The team, all sweaty and grass-stained, crowded onto the bench, where Coach Willard bawled them out again. Ginger sat nervously amid their spitting and grumbling, afraid to look up into their faces. She prayed the coach wouldn't notice her any more than the team had.

"Hi." A boy's voice breathed hot air into her hair. "Why don't you come sit with the commoners?"

Ginger drew away from Lance Woodward, who was leaning awkwardly over the bench. "I can't," she said. "I'm supposed to sit here."

Lance laughed. "I can tell. This bench will probably tip if someone doesn't hold down the end."

Ginger folded her arms and stubbornly faced the football field. "Will you please leave me alone?" She wasn't about to admit that she hated sitting here. There were certain things you had to do if you wanted to be popular in a new school.

Lance ran his fingers through his dark brown hair. "Come on. I know you're just playing hard to get."

"Ha!" Ginger hollered more loudly than she had intended. Several of the football players looked over at her. One of them wore the number twelve.

Rol's lips parted into a smile, and Ginger noticed that blood clung to one front tooth. Moon-shaped smudges covered his cheekbones. She smiled back as her pulse quickened. Rol Swenson was the cutest boy she'd ever seen, even with a dirty face. Even if Shelley thought he was weird.

Lance hung around through most of half time, leaning over Ginger, insulting her in every way he could: "Are you the manager? Why don't you fold those towels? How come you run around with that shrimp, Doylita? It looks as if you're baby-sitting. You don't like that jock, do you? I hear he's wanted in four states. Why do you . . . ?"

"Will you please *shut up!*"

Lance straightened and started to walk away as Paula Damen appeared out of nowhere.

"Hi." Paula's voice nearly cracked with excitement.

"What are you doing sitting down here?" Paula's short hair looked like a cap of shiny brown feathers. Her dark eyebrows were plucked into perfect arches and, as usual, she wore eyeshadow that matched her outfit. Today she wore a pink sweater.

"I want to hear this," Lance said sarcastically.

Ginger ignored him. "Well, you see, my locker partner is the school mascot and. . . ."

Paula's eyebrow peaked.

"She invited me to sit with her," Ginger finished.

"You haven't even called me. I thought you'd call . . . or something."

"I tried, but you're never home."

"I was home last night until five. We're still friends, aren't we?"

"Of course we're still friends."

Lance pretended to play a violin. "Tune in tomorrow for the continuing saga of Ginger and Paula, a gripping story that spans two schools. . . ."

"Will you shut up?" both girls chorused.

Paula eyed the bench. "Can I sit here with you?"

"Don't ask," Lance said. "This bench is only for important people, as you can see. Only uniforms and green skirts allowed."

Paula looked pleadingly at Ginger.

"Well, I don't know," Ginger said. "I wish you could, but we had to get permission from the coach."

"Oh." Paula's voice dropped. "That's okay. Why don't we meet after the game, then, and ride the bus home together."

Lance snickered. "She has to fold towels."

Both girls scowled at him silently until Lance said he could take a hint and left.

"The thing is," Ginger tried to explain, "I'm supposed to go to this party. To tell the truth, I'd rather go home."

"Right. I suppose it goes along with bench-sitting, huh?"

"I never said *that*!"

Paula folded her arms across the front of her fuzzy pink sweater. "You look different. You're wearing make-up." She scrutinized Ginger's face. "You're gone for one measley week, and look at you."

Ginger was indignant. "What about you? You look as if you've got pink eye."

"I do not!" Paula huffed. "I'm coordinated. Look, it's fine with me if we just forget this friendship thing."

Ginger watched her stalk away. Besides pink eye, she thought, Paula had a stupid, immature temper.

Thirty sets of cleats hammered a path across the pavement back to Alcott when the game ended. The final score was 7 to 0. The Cougars had somehow made a touchdown.

Ginger followed Doylita and the cheerleaders to Coach Willard's car, where the cake and food had been stored. Wieners, buns, potato chips, pop, and dishes covered with aluminum foil filled the back of the station wagon. Ginger's stomach rumbled at the sight of it all.

"Ooh, the cake is gorgeous." Corine leaned into the back of the car and opened the lid of the pink box. "I'm so glad we won. Now we really have something to celebrate." She threw one of her giant pompons into the air and caught it again.

Behind them a dirt-smudged team in red and white quietly loaded onto the first of three waiting school buses. Paula and the other kids who had come over from Jefferson crowded onto the other two. A girl leaned out of an open window. "Wait till next time," she yelled.

Chris waved her pompons at the girl. "We're number one!" she hollered. "Green and yellow forever!"

A chorus of boos arose from the bus.

"Jefferson rots!" Doylita yelled back. The ears on her hood bobbed.

Paula and Ginger solemnly glared at each other until the yellow caravan of buses pulled out of the parking lot. There was no doubt they were on opposite sides now. Maybe it was just as well Ginger had been transferred; red and white just didn't look right anymore.

"Come on," Doylita said. "If everyone pitches in, we can move all this stuff over to Mindy's car. Dad wants us to get everything set up before he gets there."

"Who's he bringing this time?" Mindy asked.

Doylita suddenly straightened. "No one!" Her hands went to her hips, and the face inside the cougar hood reddened. "Just because he had that stupid woman with him last time doesn't mean he's officially *dating*!"

"Okay, Doyle. Sorry." Mindy looked at Chris, who looked at Corine.

A silence followed. Then Chris reached into the back of the station wagon and loaded her arms with bags of potato chips. Janet picked up several large plastic bottles of Seven-Up. Kim reached for the cake.

"I'm carrying that!" Doylita informed her. "Here, you can take the wieners and buns."

The cheerleaders exchanged looks. Did Doylita act like this often? Ginger wondered.

A few minutes later, arriving at the Willards' house, Doylita seemed to cheer up. She tiptoed up the steps and laughed about the game. Jefferson's coach was fat, she said, and nearly bald. The plays they used were juvenile and, if they ever hoped to win, they were going to have to find a decent quarterback, not that Rol Swenson was so great.

"Hey," Ginger said. "We won, didn't we?"

Doylita fitted her key into the lock and pushed the door open.

The house was old, with white shutters and a long porch. Doylita led the group through a huge living room with an old-fashioned archway. All of the furniture looked old, with faded flowers on gray fabric, and there were newspapers and magazines lying everywhere.

The basement was the neatest part of the house, with leather chairs and tables made out of barrels.

Janet went straight to the stereo, which was built into a cabinet under the stairwell. A moment later the room rocked with music. Ginger watched Janet dance by herself in the dark corner. Doylita twirled past, still wearing her cougar costume with the hood and boots.

No one seemed nervous except Ginger, who stood in the center of the room with her box of party things. "What should I do with this stuff?" she asked.

Mindy beckoned. "Come on, I'll show you."

Ginger followed Mindy into a tiny turquoise kitchen. A little square sink fit perfectly in one corner and a two-burner stove in the other. Ginger set her box down on the yellow counter in between.

"I'll cook these," Mindy said. "if someone else will fix the buns and set the table."

"I'll be glad to help." The kitchen would be a great place to hide if she needed it, Ginger thought.

She spread a cloth over the Ping-Pong table in the other room and arranged the colored napkins in a fan shape.

Then she put out mustard, relish, and a dish of black olives, popping several olives into her mouth. She was starved, and it still irritated her that Doylita's stomach was full of doughnut holes.

Doylita personally placed the cake in the center of the table, as if it were hers alone. Ginger watched with interest. What's so great about that cake? she wondered.

Janet brought out baked beans and a potato salad her mother had made. Ginger returned to the kitchen to heat the hot-dog buns in the small oven.

This is fun, she thought, almost surprised. "Too bad the boys have to come," she said to Mindy. "We girls could have our own party."

Mindy looked shocked. "It's no fun dancing with girls. I'm going to corner Carlin Moseby the minute he comes down those stairs."

"Not me," Ginger said. "I'll be busy in the kitchen. I'm not even going to dance."

"Sure you are." Corine patted her shoulder. "There are thirty boys on the team and only seven of us girls, unless some of them bring girl friends."

Ginger pictured the scene with a sinking feeling. She hadn't thought of it that way. Maybe the boys wouldn't show up, she thought hopefully. They were awfully late already. Maybe they would stay on their own side of the room like the boys in eighth grade. Maybe they wouldn't notice her if she stayed out of their way.

Upstairs, the front door flew open, and footsteps thundered across the ceiling.

"They're here!" Corine cheered.

15.

I'm only fourteen years old, Ginger thought. I don't know what to say to boys. Panicked, she grabbed a handful of plastic forks.

The boys charged down the stairs and exploded into the room. Ginger hid just inside the kitchen doorway and watched for Rol Swenson's blond head above the others.

Finally a lean figure loped down the stairs and passed in front of Ginger.

"Hi," Rol said. His blue eyes looked into Ginger's for a second before he cut across to the Ping-Pong table where the food was spread out.

She ventured away from the doorway. "Here are the forks!" She suddenly remembered she was holding them and dashed over to the table, where she arranged them neatly in two rows.

A flurry of arms reached past her for paper plates. Corine brought a steaming panful of wieners.

"Thanks," Rol said, taking a fork.

Ginger watched him fill his paper plate with a giant heap of potato salad, two hot dogs, and a pile of yellow mustard.

Is he really going to eat all that? she wondered. Then he topped the mound off with chips and six or eight long, green pickles. The plate sagged under the weight.

It's going to fall, Ginger realized, and she reached out just in time to catch a cold blob of potato salad.

"Oops!" She looked up into Rol's pale eyes and managed an embarrassed smile. Then she stared down at the mess oozing through her fingers. What should I do with it? she wondered. She couldn't eat it; after all, it wasn't hers.

I'm going to die right in front of him, Ginger thought as her throat closed and her eyes began to water. Why do these things always happen to me? Quickly she flipped the whole mound back onto Rol's plate.

"My hands are clean," she explained.

Rol snickered. "I guess I'm kind of a klutz. Sorry."

"That's okay." Ginger hesitated, wondering where to wipe her hand.

"Here," Rol offered, setting down his loaded plate, "let me help you." He grabbed two napkins and wiped Ginger's hand, working up one finger and down the other.

She watched the shadow of his eyelashes sweep across his freckled cheeks and thought how unlike Lance Woodward he was; so thoughtful, so. . . .

She gulped and pulled her hand away. "Thanks." Ginger turned before Rol could see her red face. "I'd better go wash."

She rushed to the kitchen and ran warm water over her hand. She had never known potato salad could be so cold. But before she could even find a towel, a commotion brought her back to the doorway. She wiped her hands on her skirt.

Mr. Willard had shown up finally, and he was with a woman. Cheers and laughter filled the basement. The coach smiled at everyone, obviously in a much better mood now that Alcott had finally won a game.

Doylita pushed past Ginger into the tiny kitchen. "That sleaze! How could she?"

"Who?"

Doylita wheeled around. "Who does she think she is, acting so innocent at school all the time?"

Ginger took a second look at the woman with Doylita's father. Soft brown curls framed a thin face that seemed vaguely familiar. Ginger stared at her for several seconds before she realized who she was; Miss Stanley looked so different in the school gym.

Corine rushed into the kitchen. "They're probably just friends, Doylita. There's no reason to get upset."

Doylita's eyes glistened. "What do you know about it? She's been after him since the first day of school."

"Okay, sulk by yourself. I was just trying to help."

Corine's words stunned Doylita, who suddenly ran from the kitchen, through the basement room, and up the stairs. Ginger heard her feet progress across the ceiling into a far corner of the house. Somewhere, over the noise of the stereo, a door slammed.

"She's really getting on my nerves," Corine said to the ceiling.

"Me too," Janet said. "If it weren't for her dad, I wouldn't have anything to do with her."

Ginger turned to watch Mr. Willard hand a paper plate to Miss Stanley and fill another one for himself. He didn't seem to have noticed Doylita's tantrum.

"Hi." Rol Swenson touched Ginger's arm. "Wanna dance or anything?" His chin was smeared with mustard.

"Me?" Of course he means me, Ginger thought. "I don't dance much."

Rol extended his hand. A slow song had begun to play on the stereo. "Come on." He wiped the mustard off his chin with the back of his hand and led Ginger into the middle of the room.

Several cheerleaders waltzed out of the darkness with boys in tow. Ginger laughed as if the whole thing were a joke. What else could she do?

"Okay, but I'm not responsible for broken toes." She moved to face him, smiling as if she weren't nervous at all. His features were so pale that in the dim light she could hardly see his eyes.

Upstairs, another door slammed. Feet moved back across the ceiling.

Ginger tried to breathe normally as Rol slipped his arm around her waist and shuffled across the floor with her. She looked at the ceiling and pretended to listen for Doylita, even though Rol held her so close she could feel the warmth from his chest on her cheek.

Ginger danced on her tiptoes to reach his shoulder, her green corduroy skirt tickling the backs of her knees. Surprisingly, it didn't seem too hard to move across the floor wherever Rol led her.

The music crescendoed to an end, and Rol led her back to the wall. Ginger swallowed twice, praying she wouldn't get the hiccups from holding her breath.

Rol remained next to her with his thumbs hooked in his back pockets. Talk to him, Ginger ordered herself, but not a single thought came to her.

A few minutes later Doylita pranced into the basement again, chattering as if nothing had happened. She had changed out of her cougar outfit and was wearing a brightly striped shirt and jeans.

Ginger spotted Coach Willard and Miss Stanley sitting on a couple of barrel chairs at one of the tables, eating hot dogs.

She watched Doylita lift the cake off the Ping-Pong table and take it to them. "Ready for dessert?" Doylita asked.

Her father looked up. "The cake looks terrific, honey. Good job."

Doylita beamed as if she'd baked it herself. No wonder she had been so possessive about the cake; for once her father was smiling at her.

"I'll have a piece," Miss Stanley said.

Ginger noticed Doylita's jaw tighten as she returned the cake to the Ping-Pong table.

"Come on, everybody. Bring your plates. I'm cutting the cake." Doylita forced a smile and picked up the knife to carve six neat rows through the top, saving the plastic players on a dish. Carefully she transferred a corner piece with a high ridge of frosting onto a clean paper plate, then all but tossed a second, smaller piece onto another plate. It landed upside down and broke in two.

"I'd say Doyle's a little upset," Rol whispered.

"I know. I thought nothing ever bothered her."

Doylita smiled sweetly as she set the big piece of cake in front of her father and the other in front of Miss Stanley.

Coach Willard looked from one piece of cake to the other. "Here, Marge," he said. "I'm not too big on frosting." And he traded the plates so that Miss Stanley got the one Doylita had cut especially for her father.

Doylita stiffened.

"Thanks, honey," Coach Willard said, dismissing her.

Miss Stanley shook her head slightly and glanced at the coach. As far as Ginger could tell, he had missed the whole thing.

The mood was broken when a loud, tuneless beat blasted from the stereo. Most of the kids got up to dance, even those who had no partners. Suddenly the room came alive.

Rol clapped his hands several times. "Come on. Let's

dance." His knees bumped in and out, and his elbows flapped in rhythm with the music.

Ginger glanced nervously around the room. Mindy seemed to have gone into a frenzy, flinging her head back and forth and wiggling her shoulders.

"I don't think I can do that," Ginger said.

"It's easy," Rol said, drawing her out onto the floor. "All you do is move with the music." He danced a few feet in front of Ginger, swinging his arms and rotating his hips.

Sure, it looked easy when he did it; Rol had probably been dancing all through high school.

Ginger had no choice but to follow. She began to bounce, trying to catch the uneven rhythm with her body.

Doylita joined in and danced with several boys at once, zipping back and forth across the room.

As the record ended, Rol slid his arm around Ginger's waist. His face, with white eyelashes and pale hair, reminded her of a sunny day in December, crisp and clean.

"How come I never noticed you before this week?" Rol asked. "I usually check out all the good-looking girls."

Ginger smiled. "I transferred from Jefferson."

"Do you want to go downtown with me sometime?" he asked her.

"Well. . . ." Ginger groped for an excuse. "Actually, I've been thinking about riding the school bus from now on. I get home too late otherwise."

She pictured Doylita filling her book bag with stolen jewelry, Rol catching her in the act, and Doylita saying, "But Ginger does it, too. Just look at her shoes; she's wearing stolen pompons."

"I only walked downtown because I was afraid of getting thrown into the fountain," she admitted.

Rol laughed and tightened his grip around her waist. "I'll protect you."

Ginger held her breath. The low rumble of his voice and the feel of his touch nearly overwhelmed her. Even after he moved his arm, her waist tingled as if he were still touching her. I wouldn't mind at all if he kissed me, she thought. Not tonight, but sometime.

"I could drive you home from town." He brushed his chin across her hair.

He had a car, of course. She hadn't thought of that. Her parents would ask all kinds of questions if she showed up in a car with a boy. "You sure? I live a long way out."

"Positive." Rol turned her toward him and started to dance slowly, even though there was no music playing at the time. His blank face looked down into hers. "I suppose all the guys have told you you're gorgeous."

"Who, me?" Ginger laughed a little. "No, not exactly."

"Well, you are."

"Thanks." She let him hold her closer, and when Rol's lips touched her forehead, Ginger jolted as she felt the slight pressure of a kiss.

16.

Ginger woke early to the curtains flapping against her open window. The sunny blue sky seemed in contrast with the stiff wind that had come up during the night. She threw her covers back, flung her long legs over the edge of the bed, and ran to the open window all in one graceful motion, as if she were being filmed for a commercial. The day beamed bright and alive, a perfect match for her mood.

Closing her window, Ginger noticed the leaf-strewn yard below: orange splotches on wet, green grass. It seemed as if autumn had come overnight, like the changes in her life. Who would believe that she had only been at Alcott High School for a week?

In a way, Ginger was surprised that she had slept at all after the events of last night, with Rol still so fresh in her mind.

"Alcott High School, I love you!" Ginger sang aloud.

Saturday mornings generally meant a family breakfast of pancakes and bacon, but no one else in the house seemed to be awake.

Good, Ginger thought. Maybe she could go out for a bike ride alone, take some art supplies along, and do a few sketches. She wasn't ready for her family to invade her private thoughts. Not yet. And besides, something compelled her to be out in the elements on this particular morning.

She moved cautiously to her closet, avoiding the loose floorboard in front of her dresser, and opened the louvered doors. This wonderful day called for her favorite jeans, a plaid shirt, and thick yellow sweater.

Ginger dressed quickly, combed her hair, and tiptoed into the bathroom to brush her teeth. Then she filled a red nylon backpack with freshly sharpened pencils and a spiral sketch pad.

After descending the carpeted stairs soundlessly, she crept through the kitchen to the back door, scribbled a note on the telephone pad, picked an apple out of a wooden bowl, and let herself quietly out onto the patio. There her ten-speed bike leaned against the house.

The wind blew leaves and debris across the patio and whipped her hair into her face as she wheeled out the gate and pedaled fast down the block, heading nowhere in particular. Her ears stung from the cold air, but she didn't care. She felt healthy and beautiful.

In her mind, Ginger heard Rol's voice again and saw his white eyelashes and blue, blue eyes. Just thinking about him gave her a feeling of happiness. Does he feel the same way this morning? Ginger wondered.

She whizzed past Jefferson to Manito Park, the perfect place for sketching. She and Paula had spent practically their whole summer here, dangling their toes in the duck pond or wandering through the greenhouse, talking about the cute guys they would meet in high school. But Ginger had never pictured anyone like Rol Swenson.

With a surge of energy, she shifted into high gear and headed for the pond, where a few brave water lilies still bloomed near the shore.

A jogger in a gray sweat shirt and red headband moved to the side of the dirt path to let her by. Leaves floated out of the sky to settle silently on the grass, on the pathway, and on the brackish surface of the water.

Ginger sped toward the far end of the duck pond, then up and over a small wooden bridge. She recognized two Jefferson boys who were throwing a Frisbee back and forth, laughing when the wind carried it out of their reach. Another boy was sprawled near the water's edge in an old hooded sweat shirt. It could only be Lance Woodward, she thought.

She continued to pedal, pretending not to notice anything but the treetops and cloud-streaked sky. But from the corner of her eye she saw a huge black-and-gray goose standing a few feet from Lance with its long neck stretched toward his hand. As Ginger coasted by, the goose let forth a loud honk. She jerked to a stop. The goose flapped its wings and waddled into the water.

Lance turned abruptly. "Good going! I almost had her."

Ginger scowled. "You mean you were trying to catch that poor thing?"

"I was trying to feed her," Lance retorted. "I've almost got her eating out of my hand." He looked from Ginger's face to her shoe pompons and back again.

"What are you doing here?" He brightened. "Looking for me?"

Ginger ignored his question and asked, "How do you know it's a she?"

"By the way she walks," Lance said. He sat up and rested his elbows on his knees.

"I don't see anything wrong with the way she walks."

Lance looked down and played with a dandelion so long Ginger thought he had forgotten about her. "How come you're always running around with those scums at school?"

"They're not scums." Does he know about Doylita and her shoplifting? she wondered.

"I've been around more than you have," Lance said. "I'm telling you they're all jerks. Take that jock, Rol What's-his-name. . . ."

"Rol Swenson is nice. Besides, I wouldn't talk after all the trouble you've been in."

"That was then. This is now."

95

Ginger opened her mouth to say something more, then gave up. There was no use arguing with someone like Lance.

She shoved hard on the pedal of her bike and whizzed away, knowing she'd get another smart remark from behind her. Lance would probably die if he didn't have the last word.

"Hey, that's a sexy sweater!"

The front wheel of Ginger's bike wobbled off the path, nearly causing her to run over a brown duck nestled in the grass. It quacked frantically and flew the short distance to the pond.

Ginger's face burned, but she refused to look back.

"Just watch what you're doing!" she hollered at the duck.

Feeling deflated, Ginger returned home without sketching a thing. What did Lance know about Rol Swenson, anyway? He was probably just jealous.

The following Friday, in the midst of a cold drizzle, Shelley Franklin stood on the concrete ledge outside the front doors at Alcott, a load of books in her arms, and looked down at Gary Goodwin who waited below. Two other boys grabbed at her from the top step.

"You're doomed," one of them said. "May as well go peaceably."

Shelley screamed and backed up until her shoulders pressed against the red brick of the school building. "No way!" she cried. "You're not getting me into that fountain! I'll freeze to death." She spit at him, but she only reached the bottom step.

Ginger looked down at Doylita, who bounced along beside her, unruffled by the latest outbreak of dunkings.

More than a week had gone by since Mr. Wintermeyer had warned the students against using the fountain as a swimming pool, and Ginger had almost begun to relax.

"Tell them to stop," she said to Doylita. "That's Shelley."

"You tell them." Doylita grinned on one side of her mouth. "No one ever died from getting wet."

"Doylita! It's cold," Ginger said and hugged her coat to her neck. "How would *you* feel with wet hair and mascara running down your face?" She watched nervously as Shelley debated which way to jump.

Ginger stood torn between running back into the school for the principal and helping Shelley herself. What can I do? she wondered. It won't help Shelley if we both get drenched.

Just then the big double doors to the building flew open and out walked Rol. Ginger sighed with relief. He'll put a stop to this silliness, she thought proudly.

Rol looked at Shelley, then down at the fountain and at another girl who stood on the rim shivering and hugging herself. He smiled broadly and let out an elated howl. In one quick motion he snatched Shelley off the rail and draped her over his shoulder.

Ginger gasped. Doylita doubled over laughing. Shelley screamed and clawed at Rol's back as he strode with her down the stairs toward the fountain.

Ginger's face flushed as anger mounted inside her. What was he doing picking up a girl he hardly knew? And she had thought he was too nice to do such things!

"Rol, stop!" Ginger heard herself yell. "Put her down!" She dropped her book bag and ran toward the pair.

Shelley looked up from where she dangled down Rol's back. "Help!"

"Rol Swenson, you put her down right this minute! Shelley is a friend of mine!"

Rol turned in midstride, swinging Shelley and her long braid in a wide arc. Her glasses fell off onto the grass.

His face registered surprise at seeing Ginger. "You're no fun," he complained.

"Will you pl-ease put me down?" Shelley screamed, beating on Rol's back. "I'm going to be sick." She coughed.

Rol quickly bent down and slid Shelley off his shoulder. "Not on me, you're not."

Shelley picked up her glasses and ran for the school steps. "I don't know what you see in that creep!" she screamed at Ginger. Shelley was crying.

Ginger looked on with dismay. Rol seemed so different all of a sudden. She crossed her arms. "That was really a rotten thing to do!"

Rol turned toward her and laughed. "Hey, you're even prettier when you're mad!"

"I am not!"

"Yes, you are. Come on, let's go downtown." He reached for her hand.

Ginger softened. "I don't know."

"Come on."

She turned to Doylita. "Is it okay with you?" Ginger tried not to smile but couldn't help herself.

"Sure," Doylita said. "Let's go."

Six kids piled into Rol's red Camaro. Mindy, Carlin, and John sat in the back seat. Ginger slid into the front seat next to Rol and Doylita took the last space near the door. Rol drove one-handed, with an arm draped around Ginger. She looked at his hand dangling near her chin and a smile tugged at the corner of her mouth.

17

The minute the group moved through the doors at Freman's, Ginger spotted a Halloween display set up on a long table covered with a shiny black cloth.

"Ooh, gross!" John yelled, and the boys all raced over to get a closer look. Rol drew his arm away from Ginger and charged through the aisle with them.

Mannequin heads, made up to look like monsters, sat on little shelves of different heights. Some wore ghoulish rubber masks. Packages of fake vampire blood and goop for scars were piled around the base. Cards of long, green fingernails and fanglike teeth hung on spindles next to the table.

Carlin made claws out of his hands and screwed up his face. "Hey, cool. I'm getting some of this stuff." He stalked toward Doylita, who giggled and ducked out of his way.

Ginger circled the tables examining each of the heads. Cotton balls formed scabs all over one of the faces with a single eyeball set in the middle.

The kids all laughed and pointed to their favorite faces, saying they looked like Alcott teachers.

"That's Mr. Clarke." Ginger pointed to arched eyebrows and a thick, black mustache on a bluish face.

Rol clutched her hand and laughed. "Dracula. That's Clarke, all right." His fingers wiggled against hers, and Ginger leaned against his arm. Heat radiated right through his jacket onto her cheeks.

Doylita had separated from the group and was looking

at a rack of watchbands. Ginger smiled, hoping to catch her attention. But then her heart dropped into her stomach. There was something familiar about the way Doylita stood so close to the counter, handling the watchbands and glancing up at the saleslady every few seconds.

Ginger pulled her hand away from Rol and wiped her damp palm on her jeans. He looked down momentarily, then turned to Carlin. Doylita hadn't stolen anything all week. Why today? She's going to get caught, Ginger thought nervously.

She looked up into Rol's face and then at the big hands that held tubes of green make-up and cards of false fingernails. She nearly sighed out loud. She'd never known a boy like him before. What would he think if he knew about the doughnut holes she'd almost taken and about the pompons she was wearing?

She had nearly decided to rush over and stop Doylita when she noticed Rol's left hand disappear into the front of his jacket—one quick motion, as if he were putting away a checkbook—and when it came out again it was empty. He held no make-up or fingernails. Or anything.

Oh, no! Not Rol, too! Ginger's eyes open wide in disbelief. She scanned the table quickly. Surely the items were lying there somewhere! He couldn't really have ripped them off.

Only the vampire blood and the scar goop were piled on the table. The other things all hung neatly on spindles. Ginger's eyes glistened, and she turned away as Rol zipped his jacket almost to his neck. A sob forced its way out of her throat. Not Rol Swenson!

Ginger closed her eyes tightly, and she edged down the aisle, past Doylita, toward the big front doors of Freman's. Why did he have to do it now, after he had made her believe he was so wonderful? Ginger walked faster. What a fake!

"Where are you going?" Rol asked from behind her.

"Nowhere," she answered flatly.

"What's the matter?"

"Nothing."

"Yes, there is. What's wrong?"

He doesn't even know, Ginger thought with disgust. Tell him off, she commanded herself, but she could not seem to find her voice. Instead she stopped short, allowing Rol to turn her around and guide her toward the escalator.

"Come on. We're going to check out the ski clothes."

The entire crowd of kids followed, including Doylita, who probably had a whole bag full of watchbands. She doesn't even wear a watch, Ginger thought sadly.

A saleslady relaxed against a counter as the group stepped onto the escalator.

Ginger rode up in a daze, aware only of her misery and of Rol's arm around her. Could it be true that *everyone* ripped things off? Why hadn't she believed Doylita, who always seemed to know what was going on? What made Ginger so different, such a goody-goody? Doylita, and now Rol, both shoplifted. Who else? she wondered.

It seemed an eternity before the group gathered on the sidewalk outside of Freman's. At last the muscles in Ginger's shoulders relaxed and she exhaled a long breath. Why am I so relieved? she wondered. It would serve them both right if they got caught. But she had watched the front of Rol's jacket for the past hour, terrified that a card of fingernails would fall out.

Ginger felt sick inside. The world seemed to have

turned upside down. She would expect something like this of Lance Woodward. After all, he was the *type*. Not Rol Swenson.

But it wasn't the stolen fingernails that bothered Ginger the most; it was her own confusion. There were good guys and there were bad guys. Ginger had always identified with the heroes. Now she could only register disgust with herself for being so naive.

She knew Rol had faults, but did it really matter so much? Maybe there was something wrong with *her*.

And there was one other thing that made a difference now. Upstairs, between the socks and the men's belts, he had asked her to go to the Halloween dance with him.

Rol had touched her hair and said, "Hey, if you're going to be so glum, I'll have to take someone else to the Halloween dance."

"I'm not glum," she had said. "I'm just upset . . . about something."

"Well, do you think you could get over it by the twenty-ninth? That's the last Friday of the month."

Ginger smiled, even though she hadn't wanted to. "I guess so."

Now, outside of Freman's, Rol stood with one arm draped around Ginger while he unzipped his jacket.

"Anybody need any green make-up?" he asked, laughing.

The sight of it sickened Ginger all over again, but she fought to remain casual, as if her heart were beating at its normal rate.

Doylita reached into her bag and started passing things out to everyone in the group: watchbands for the girls, cuff links and ball-point pens for the boys. Ginger watched in amazement. No one else seemed surprised.

"Doylita, you're really ba-ad," Mindy said. "How'd you get all that stuff?"

Doylita wiggled her fingers. "It's called manual dexterity."

"You got any TV sets in that bag?" Carlin asked. The others laughed.

Ginger dropped the things Doylita had given her into her own book bag. It seemed easier than arguing in front of everyone. No one else seemed to be worried about it, so why should she worry?

18.

"Have you seen my Furry Burry?" Mark poked his head into Ginger's room one day late in October.

She jerked her hand out of her dresser drawer and stood up straight. "Will you please knock after this? You scared me half to death!"

Mark's lips tightened into a thin line. "You took my bear. I know you did."

"Why would I want your stupid bear? If I were you, I'd be ashamed to admit I even had one. Now, will you get out of here. I'm busy."

Mark pulled the door closed with an angry bang. "I'm telling," he threatened. "You're the only one around here mean enough. . . ." His voice trailed off as he descended the stairs.

It was true. Ginger had felt mean ever since Rol had stolen the make-up. But there was no one to talk to, no one who would understand. She reached into her dresser drawer and smoothed her underwear over the items Doylita had given her.

Just before dinner her mother came into her room with a load of clean, folded clothes. Ginger jumped up off her bed, suddenly alarmed.

"Here, Mom. I'll take them!"

"Ginger, is something wrong? You seem so fidgety lately."

Ginger took the clothes and stuffed them all—jeans, panties, socks—into the same bottom drawer.

"I'm fine," Ginger told her mother. "It's just the new school . . . and everything."

"Well, I'd like you to come on down and set the table."

"Why can't Mark do it?" Ginger retorted, surprised at her own sharp voice.

Her mother hesitated in the doorway with a puzzled look on her face. "Because . . . your brother takes out the garbage and mows the lawn *and* keeps his room neat." She folded her arms and looked around at Ginger's messy surroundings.

Her mother was right, Ginger knew, but at that moment a strange kind of sadness swelled in her chest and she couldn't stop herself from saying, "Sure, Mark is perfect."

"I always thought you were *both* practically perfect," Mrs. Wilson said, sounding hurt. "Come on, what's wrong?"

"You hate me!" Ginger persisted, her eyes brimming with inexplicable tears.

"Ginger, you know perfectly well that isn't true." Her mother sighed. "Maybe you'll feel better after dinner. Come on down and set the table." Mrs. Wilson waited for a second, then pulled the door firmly closed behind her.

Ginger drove her fist into her pillow, but the only sound was an unsatisfying "puff."

She pushed her bathrobe and some magazines aside and stretched out on top of her rumpled quilt. One of her blankets was pink with electric cords running through, and under that lay an old army blanket she'd had just about forever. Where had it come from? Why had she never thought about it before? Ginger tucked the lace pillow under her chin and watched wet circles form where her tears dripped. Her father must have taken the blanket years ago when he was at Fort Devens.

Stealing was all around her. Everyone did it, just as Doylita had said. Even sampling grapes at the grocery store was stealing in a way, so her mother was a thief, too.

She fingered the drab old blanket, trying to picture her father sneaking it out of the army barracks.

After a while, she got up and headed for the kitchen. On the way down the stairs she tried to fix a cheerful expression on her face. One thing she didn't want was anyone asking more questions about her mood, especially when no one cared anyway.

But during dinner Ginger listened quietly while her parents discussed her. Why couldn't they just let it drop?

"Not only that, her room's been a mess for weeks," Mrs. Wilson was saying.

Hello, I'm sitting right here, Ginger wanted to remind them.

"Well, it's tough changing schools," he father put in with a smile in Ginger's direction. "Her grades are up. It looks to me as if she's adjusting okay."

"I don't know," her mother said.

Ginger looked off into space. If they were going to treat her as though she wasn't even here, then she wouldn't *be* here.

"You would come to us if you had a problem, wouldn't you?"

Ginger jumped as her mother touched her arm. "Huh? Yeah, I guess so."

Mark, who had been watching faces all through dinner as if there were a Ping-Pong match going on, finally entered the conversation. "I know one thing; my bear's been missing for two weeks."

It's been missing longer than that, Ginger thought, and felt that familiar twinge of meanness.

"Oh, I almost forgot. I've been invited to a Halloween dance at school. It's the twenty-ninth. I can go, can't I?"

"Really?" Her mother seemed happy to change the subject. "That sounds like fun."

"Boy or girl?" her father asked.

Ginger flushed and clutched her napkin. "Well, a boy. But it's not exactly a date. It's an afternoon dance. Right after school."

Her parents looked at each other and nodded their permission.

"Just don't have too much fun." Her father laughed.

Ginger forced a smile. What did they think she was going to do?

It wasn't until Wednesday, when Mr. Clarke read the bulletin, that Ginger found out the Halloween dance was to be a costume party.

Costumes? Ginger looked desperately toward Doylita. Costumes in high school? The last time Ginger had dressed up, she had gone trick-or-treating as Bugs Bunny. No way would she dance with Rol looking so stupid.

"Do we *have* to wear costumes?"

"I guess so," Ellen Warneke said.

"That's the dumbest thing I've ever heard," Ginger said. "I hate costumes!" What could she wear? Maybe she could go as a teen-ager in comfortable jeans. Cute. Of course, Rol would be wearing a Dracula costume; he'd already stolen half of it.

Frantically Ginger went through the closets at home, throwing things onto the floor, trying to come up with a clever idea.

From the back of the hall closet she pulled out her old Bugs costume with the fuzzy ears and the footie pajamas her mother had remade. No. They were out! The ears looked shabby and the pajamas too small.

The only other thing she found was an old tutu. No way!

"What about that clown costume your grandmother made?" Mrs. Wilson suggested.

"That old thing? I wouldn't be seen in that!"

"All right. Suit yourself." Her mother gave up and went back into the kitchen.

Mark bumped down the stairs on the seat of his pants. "I know what you could be," he said.

"What? No, don't tell me," Ginger amended. "I don't even want to hear what you're thinking."

"It's a real good idea."

Ginger looked at him, almost trusting him, but not quite. Still, she *was* desperate. "Okay, but this had better be good."

Mark smiled. "It's simple. Go as a bunny."

"You dumbbell. That was the first thing I thought of."

She picked up the old pajamas. "Just how do you think I would get into these things? Not that I would want to."

Her brother stood up. "Not that kind of bunny." He picked up the ears. "I mean the kind who works in a restaurant."

Ginger brightened. "Hey, yeah. I could wear these ears—" she took them from Mark and tied them on her head—"and my ballet tights and leotard. I don't believe it; you had a good idea for the first time in your life."

Mark frowned. "You're welcome," he said.

For a second Ginger felt sorry for him, but she was suddenly too busy to apologize. She took the stairs two at a time and closed herself into her room, where she tried on the entire costume, then stood looking at herself in the full-length mirror. The high-heeled shoes were missing— but that was all—to make this a perfect costume.

"Mom," she called down the stairs. "Can I borrow your Christmas shoes, the silver ones with the high heels?"

Mrs. Wilson came up the stairs and into Ginger's room. Looking her daughter over from head to toe, she said in a worried voice, "It's kind of brief, isn't it?"

"What do you mean?"

"Well . . . you're going to freeze to death."

Ginger's shoulders drooped. She was too tired to think of anything else; besides, Mark had had a good idea. "Mom, this is the same thing I used to wear to ballet. What's the difference?"

"The difference is, you're a lot older now."

Ginger turned away from the mirror. "It's just a costume. All the kids will be dressed up. Can I borrow your shoes? Please?"

Mrs. Wilson reluctantly left and returned with the silver shoes.

Wobbling and hanging onto the doorknob for support, Ginger strapped the shoes on and looked at herself again in the mirror.

Perfect, she thought, as she adjusted the ears. Almost. If only these things weren't so old and limp. The ears didn't even stand up. But Rol would like the costume. She ran her hands down her slim waist and hips.

Her mother watched as if she could change her mind at any moment. "Well, be sure to wear a sweater," she said.

19.

Doylita leaned impatiently against the row of lockers on Thursday and watched Ginger put on her coat. "Let's go," she coaxed. "I want to get some things for my costume."

"What are you wearing?" Ginger asked her and slammed the locker door shut.

"I'm not telling. It's a surprise." Doylita grinned from one side of her mouth as the two walked away. "But I'll give you a hint. I need cardboard and felt pens. Lots of 'em."

Ginger matched Doylita's quick pace out of the school and down the walk. Cardboard and felt pens didn't sound like much of a costume, but knowing Doylita, Ginger knew it would be something spectacular, something no one else in the world would ever come up with.

"Just tell me this much," Ginger asked. "Will your eyes be showing?"

Doylita laughed. "One clue is all you get. What are you going to wear?"

"Just some old things I had at home. You'll see."

They entered Freman's ahead of the crowd, and Doylita left Ginger standing near the Halloween masks while she skirted the aisles to the rear of the store.

"Don't watch, now."

"I won't." Ginger turned her back and picked up a curly red wig off a table that was piled high with things to transform little kids into insects, animals, superheroes, and clowns. Ginger tossed the red wig back and picked up a furry cat's tail with ears to match.

I'll bet they have bunny ears, Ginger thought as she pushed aside a stack of plastic ladybug shells. A spot of pink showed at the very bottom of the pile and she pulled out a cellophane package of pink-and-white plush. Seeing that it wasn't sealed, she dumped the contents out in front of her and fingered two white ears lined with pink satin and a round wad of pink fluff that was a bunny tail.

Ginger squeezed it and felt the tail expand in her hand. "Oh, it's so cute," she said out loud and knew that somehow she had to have these things for her costume.

She dropped the pink ball back on the pile. What was she thinking? She didn't have any money. Well, so what! If Doylita or Rol were here they would simply take anything they wanted.

Ginger looked nervously around her. The usual wave of kids had not come into the store yet. No one stood anywhere near the Halloween displays. Not even a salesclerk.

She dropped her book bag and held the clean, white ears up to her head, then peered across the aisle into a mirror on the make-up counter. The ears stood up in two sharp, white peaks.

There must be a way, Ginger thought with resolution. She only needed the things for one day. Maybe she could return them after the dance. What difference would it make? The tail and ears would still be just like new. No one would care.

Ginger swallowed, feeling as if she were halfway down a slide. The hollows under her arms grew damp. Oh, for heaven's sake, stop being such a goody-goody, she scolded herself.

She took a deep breath and let it out again. Then Ginger knocked some costume parts onto the floor, including a brand-new package of bunny ears and tail, and stooped to pick them up. Doylita had gotten away with four pairs of socks in the same way and no one had suspected a thing.

Quickly Ginger scooped everything up again, except for one cellophane package, which she stuffed up into her coat. All she had to do now was stand up, drop her armload on the table, and walk away. Ginger exhaled, feeling vaguely proud of herself. In another minute she would be free. Wouldn't Rol laugh if he could see her now? Doylita, too. She couldn't stop a smile from curling her lips.

And then it happened.

As Ginger was squatting near the table a pair of men's shoes walked up and stood next to her. Gray trousers led upward to a red tie and a man's face. Her head suddenly buzzed with disconnected thoughts: where did he come from? The system never worked this way for Doylita. Why is he wearing a red tie for Halloween?

Ginger held her arm tightly against her coat. Maybe she could just stand up and let the package fall out, as if she had never seen it before.

"I'll have to ask you to come into the back room with

me," the man said solemnly. He was her father's age, with black hair and a bristly mustache.

Ginger stood up awkwardly and tried not to look down when the cellophane package slid to the carpet next to her shoe. She gasped, near tears, and groped for the words to explain what she had just done.

"Glunk . . . ," she managed to say before her throat closed.

The man's mouth went into a tight line as he picked up the package and tucked it under his arm.

"I've never done anything like this before," she rushed to say, but the man ignored her remark and guided her roughly by the elbow toward a curtained doorway.

Faces appeared out of nowhere to watch her move by. Blinded by embarrassment, Ginger saw the world spin in a multicolored blur. If only she could faint or go invisible. What am I going to tell my dad? she wondered. He would say she had gone over the cliff with the sheep.

Sweat prickled on her forehead. What would happen to her now? Fine time to think of *that*, her father would say. She wanted to cry but knew it wouldn't do any good. Her brain felt like a fuzzy hole; not a single plan came to her.

Doylita would know what to do, what to say. "I have to find my friend," Ginger declared in desperation and tried to turn away as the man nudged her through the curtain.

He let go of her arm for a moment. "What does she look like? Which way did she go?"

"She's real little, with blond hair. I think she's getting some felt-tip pens."

In the back room a teen-aged boy sat on the floor, putting together a doll buggy. A fresh wave of humiliation came over Ginger as she stared at his face. She'd never seen him before, so why did she care what he thought of her? He held his screwdriver midturn as he stared back.

A gray-haired woman worked at a desk with some papers and an adding machine. She looked up and sighed as if she knew right away what was going on.

"I got you a shoplifter, Irene," the man said. Looking away, the boy twisted the screwdriver. "Her friend got away. I'll see if I can catch her."

"Doylita didn't . . . do anything," Ginger started to say, but the man had already rushed off.

Irene swiveled her chair. "Another shoplifter. I don't know where you kids get off thinking you're entitled to anything you want. It's hardly worth being in business sometimes." She opened her top drawer, tore a printed form off a thick pad, and started to ask questions.

"What's your name?"

Ginger glanced at the boy with the doll buggy. "Ginger Wilson." The words came out in a whisper.

"What? Speak up."

She cleared her throat. "Ginger Wilson."

"Address?" By her tone the woman didn't seem to care what Ginger had taken or why. Maybe this was the insurance form Doylita had mentioned.

Ginger relaxed, but only a little. "Twelve-sixteen Belmont Drive."

"Telephone?"

"Five-five-five, two-seven-five-two."

"I think we'd better give your folks a call."

Ginger's heart nearly stopped. Why would they have to call her parents for insurance? she wondered. "No one's home," she explained quickly, and she prayed it was true.

The boy stood up, tested the doll buggy by moving it

back and forth, and left through the curtain. At the same time, the mustached man walked in with Doylita.

Ginger's breath caught in her throat. All those times Doylita had said, "It's no big deal. The stores expect you to take things," she hadn't even believed it herself. There stood Doylita, looking smaller than usual, with her face all red and wet from crying.

"I didn't do anything," Doylita whined. "I want to go home."

Ginger stared in disbelief. What was going on?

Irene touched Doylita's hair softly and said, "No one's going to hurt you. Now, what's your name, honey?"

"Su-san (sob) Fos-ter."

Ginger rolled her eyes toward the ceiling. Doylita knew what to say all right.

"How old are you, dear?"

"Ten."

Ten? She was fourteen, the same as Ginger! Did she really expect them to believe her? Irene wrote down the number.

The man still held the package that had fallen out of Ginger's coat, and now he dropped it on the desk. "This is what the older one got; rabbit ears."

Irene shot a look of contempt at Ginger and turned back to Doylita. "You have nothing to worry about, honey, as long as you didn't take anything. Let's see what you have in your bag, here." She dumped the contents out on the desk.

Ginger looked down at a make-up purse, some folded papers, several gum wrappers, and six or eight yellow felt-tipped pens. Open the purse, Ginger wanted to say, no ten-year-old carries eye shadow. But Irene seemed only to see the new pens.

114

Doylita continued to sob, her small body heaving in and out like an accordion under her jacket. "I didn't do anything," she repeated.

You're making me sick, Ginger wanted to say.

Irene and the man exchanged looks. He picked up one of the pens and turned it over in his hand.

Doylita sniffed loudly. A silver column of drool hung from her chin to the front of her jacket. How did she *do* that? "I was going to pay for them," Doylita said in a small voice, "but I couldn't find a saleslady."

"Here." Irene pushed a box of Kleenex toward her. "You shouldn't have put the pens in your book bag. It looked as if you were planning to steal them."

Doylita blew her nose. "I won't do it again," she promised, looking at the woman from under her dark eyelashes.

"All right. We'll let it go this time, but I want to talk to your friend for a while. Can you get home on your own?"

"Yes." Doylita nodded and wiped at her eyes. Ginger noticed a smudge of mascara on the Kleenex, but no one else saw it. Ten years old! Ha!

"You run along, then," Irene said.

Doylita turned and left quickly with a lopsided grin at Ginger. Her tears had dried like magic. Who would believe the truth, that the two girls were the same age and that it had been Doylita who had taught Ginger how to shoplift? No one, that's who; Ginger was nearly twice Doylita's size, for one thing. And Ginger couldn't very well use the excuse that she had planned to pay for the ears and tail, not when they had been stuffed inside her coat; besides, she'd already confessed.

"I was just going to borrow them," Ginger said lamely.

20.

"Uh-huh," the man said, as if he didn't believe her. "Do you want me to call Sergeant Barclay, Irene?"

Sergeant? Ginger squirmed and reached for a metal chair. "May I sit down, please?" Without waiting for an answer, she allowed her legs to buckle under her and sank into the chair. They couldn't call the police for one little pair of bunny ears, could they?

Irene hesitated over the form. "Exactly where did you say you stopped her, Mel?"

"Next to the Halloween displays. One of the customers tipped me off."

A shiver crawled across Ginger's scalp; someone had been watching her.

"You mean she hadn't left the area?"

"No, not yet."

The woman tapped her pencil against the paper and thought for a minute. What was going on?

"The police won't come down here for this, not when she didn't leave the store I'm going to have to let her go." Irene turned to Ginger, who suddenly straightened. "Is this the first time you've stolen anything?"

"Yes. I mean, I wasn't going to steal the ears. I just thought maybe I could use them once and then bring them back." Ginger's words sounded ridiculous even to herself.

"It's stealing, nevertheless," Irene said crossly. "Do you understand that?"

Ginger nodded her shame, though she was beginning to feel hopeful. *If I somehow get out of this, I'll be good* the rest of my life, she bargained toward the ceiling. How could she have been so stupid?

"You may not think so now," Irene said, "but you're lucky to have gotten caught early." The woman almost smiled. "Now, if I let you go, I don't want to see you in this store again. Is that clear?"

"Yes," Ginger said simply. Relief washed over her like a nice, cool breeze. She stood up quickly.

"As for your friend, she's young and impressionable. If you bring her downtown with you again, I hope you'll behave yourself."

Ginger cringed. If only she dared to tell the truth, but it was no use. The woman had already decided that Ginger was the crook.

Mel held the curtain back, and Ginger passed by him. "Thanks." Her real name's Doylita, she ached to say. But even the name sounded improbable.

With her eyes fixed on the beige carpet, Ginger rushed through the store, feeling like an animal that had just been uncaged. She rounded the corner where the escalator rolled out of the floor, hurried past the watch cases, and made her way toward the front doors.

Girls crowded around the make-up counters. Several boys from Alcott were laughing and pushing each other into racks of coats. Kids milled noisily in the aisles, touching everything as if the feel itself was some kind of thrill. Ginger would never again be part of this scene.

I'm going to ask Shelley if I can still get on the basketball team, she thought. I can take the city bus when it goes by the school. If I get thrown into the fountain . . . I guess I'll live. Ginger wiggled her shoulders and forced herself to relax.

But as she was leaving the store, her heart again

skittered in her chest. Behind a counter of beer steins, men's umbrellas, and manicure sets, Mr. Clarke stood unpacking a box of old-fashioned shaving mugs.

"Well, Miss Wilson."

At first Ginger didn't recognize him outside the chemistry lab. She looked again. "Oh, Mr. Clarke! What are you doing here?"

"Working part time for Christmas." His face grew serious. "Is anything wrong?"

Ginger's hand went to a hot cheek. "No, I'm fine. It's just that . . . I'm in a hurry."

"You mean, I can't sell you anything?" Black silk snapped tight as he opened an umbrella over his head. His teeth gleamed in an exaggerated smile. "Wanna buy an umbrella?"

Ginger forced a laugh. "Uh, no, thanks. I really gotta go." Rudely she turned and rushed out the front doors into a light sprinkling of rain. Did he know what she'd done? Nothing got past Mr. Clarke at school.

Ginger zipped her coat and ducked under a ledge extending the length of the store, then turned the corner and headed straight for the bus stop. In an hour she would be home, where someone still loved her. I'll give Mark his bear, she resolved, feeling a little better.

Doylita waited in the shadows under the eaves. "Hey, Ginger. How'd it go?" A bright, innocent smile covered her face. The redness of her nose had faded. Doylita looked perfectly normal, not like a ten-year-old who had just gotten into trouble.

A bus pulled up, the wrong one, but Ginger boarded anyway and took a seat on the far side. She did not want to speak to Doylita again now, maybe never.

Two transfers and an hour later, Ginger trudged home

from the bus stop in a steady rain. The night was thick and dark. Her hair hung limply over her shoulders as if she had been doused in the fountain. The pompons on her shoes sat wet and lifeless.

Had this been the worst day of her life? She thought back to her first day at Alcott and to the day she had gotten the transfer notice. Maybe tomorrow would be even worse when everyone at school found out that Ginger Wilson had been caught shoplifting.

Shoplifting. The word itself sounded criminal. And her sentence would last the rest of her life; she could never go into Freman's again.

Suddenly the impact of that reality hit her. Pictures of herself as a grown woman with a little girl of her own swam through her mind. She saw herself standing outside of Freman's wishing she could go in, then finally taking the child by the hand and crossing the street to shop somewhere else. Irene would be very old by then, but she would remember everything.

The lights in the Wilson house glowed warmly as Ginger reached the porch outside. She could see through the living room window to the fire her father had lit. Mark was sprawled on the floor and her mother was in the kitchen putting something in the microwave.

A feeling of love for her family, even Mark, gripped Ginger unexpectedly. She tiptoed off the porch and walked around the side of the house to the back gate. Water spilled out of the gutters overhead to splash on the fence.

She ducked and entered the backyard where she looked up at Mark's bedroom window. Where was Furry Burry? He wasn't on the ledge where she left him. Maybe Mark had finally found the bear and taken him in.

She pushed a thicket of dead dahlias out of the way to

check in the flower bed. A dark lump lay next to the concrete foundation, not looking like a stuffed animal at all.

Ginger reached through a screen of spider webs and pulled the bear out.

"Poor thing," she heard herself say as she hugged the lump to her. He wasn't wet really, just cold and misshapen. She pushed on the side of his head and squeezed his body. No telling how long he'd been lying on the ground. She patted him and raked at his brown fur with her fingers, then pushed Furry Burry down into her book bag.

"You'll be in the house where it's warm in just a minute," she told the bear.

Ginger wiped her feet on the back-porch mat and went in. "I'm home," she called, hoping her voice sounded perfectly normal. "I'll change my clothes and be down in a minute. I'm soaked," she explained, as she hurried through the kitchen and up the stairs. Ginger sensed three pair of eyes following her. Her mother said something, but Ginger didn't hear what it was.

Stopping in her brother's bedroom first, she carefully placed Furry Burry under Mark's bed with one paw sticking out from under the bedspread. Then she escaped to her own room and switched on the light.

Ginger's eyes riveted on her bed, where a cellophane package of pink-and-white fur lay innocently on top of her quilt. Her hand went to her mouth as if it were attached to a spring. Was she in the Twilight Zone? How could these ears and tail have followed her home?

21.

Ginger blinked, but the package stayed on the bed. Her mind raced. How had it gotten there? Irene must have been to the house . . . or something.

Her hand was still on the doorknob when her mother came up behind her. "Ginger, there's something I want to discuss. Here it is after five again; I'm just not comfortable with your coming home so late. From now on I want you to take the bus, okay? I'm sure in this cold weather, the fountain. . . ."

Ginger looked at her mother but saw only the bunny ears and tail. "Yeah, okay."

"I know you're growing up and need more freedom, but the thing is. . . ."

"I said okay, Mom." She pointed toward the bed. "Where did that package come from?"

Her mother looked down and smiled. "I bought you some new ears for your costume. Why don't you try them on?" She studied Ginger's face. "What's the matter? You look so tired. You aren't sick, are you?"

"No, I'm fine." Ginger's mouth had gone so dry that her tongue seemed to stick to the roof of her mouth.

She went to her bed and opened the package, being careful not to look directly at her mother. "Did you get these at Freman's?" She held her breath.

"Uh-huh. I met Mrs. Damen for lunch."

At least she and her mother hadn't been there at the same time; that was lucky. Ginger ran her finger along the length of one of the soft ears. She didn't even want to go to the dance anymore, especially not as a bunny.

"I've been thinking . . . Grandma really would be happy if I wore the clown costume she made." Ginger looked up hopefully at her mother, whose smile had fallen from her face.

"Ginger, I paid seven ninety-eight for those things! It's a little late to be changing your mind. You can't return Halloween costumes, you know. The lady who sold me the ears said that kids 'borrow' things like that, use them once, and then try to return them for cash. Can you imagine?"

Ginger squirmed. Her armpits turned on and her face burned. She knows, Ginger thought.

Mrs. Wilson looked at her daughter, puzzled. "Are you sure there isn't anything wrong?"

"Hey, Mom!" Mark screamed from the next room. "I found my bear! He was under my bed all the time!" He charged out of his room and pushed Ginger's door open. His face positively glowed.

Ginger avoided the knowing stare of her mother, who folded her arms and raised one eyebrow. Why was it that everything she did backfired on her?

Her mind was so preoccupied with worry the next morning that she walked right up to the bus stop and stood in front of the Scotch broom.

She scowled at Lance, who fell back against the utility pole. "What? No wheezing or sneezing? Have you had the cure?" he asked. The two girls hadn't shown up yet.

"Huh?"

"The Scotch broom. You're allergic, remember?"

Ginger felt as if she were going to explode. The bunny costume was in the bottom of her book bag. She didn't want to go to the dance. She didn't want to face Doylita at school. And she didn't want to fight with Lance. She looked up at him and tears suddenly clouded her vision.

"What'd *I* say?" Lance lifted his shoulders in a giant, helpless shrug. "Women. You're all crazy."

"Look, yesterday was absolutely the worst day of my life. Okay? So just leave me alone for once."

"Yeah, sure, okay. What happened?"

Ginger sniffed several times. She ached to tell someone. And Lance had probably been in worse trouble himself. "I got caught . . . shoplifting."

His mouth sprang open, then he threw his head back and laughed. "You? I don't believe it! What'd you take?"

"I'm not going to tell you."

"Why not?"

"Just because." Lance would never stop laughing if he found out she had nearly ruined her life over a pair of fur ears and a tail. "Doylita took something, too; but she told them she was only ten years old, and they let her go. She steals all the time."

"She'll get caught sooner or later," Lance said certainly.

The girls showed up just before the bus came rattling along, and the foursome climbed aboard. Ginger sat with Shelley and confessed the whole story. "Please don't tell anyone else, though. I feel bad enough as it is."

"You can trust me," Shelley said. "And I don't think Doylita will mention it either. She can't be too proud of herself, acting like such a baby."

"After last night, I don't care if I ever see her again. I sure wish she weren't my locker partner."

"Why don't you move out?" Shelley said, as she gave her braid a twist.

Ginger hadn't thought of that. "You mean, to a locker

by myself? But there weren't any more. That's why I got put in with Doylita."

"Maybe not for your homeroom. But there might be someplace else. Kids changed all the time at Fairview."

Ginger considered the idea all the way to school, and during lunch she stopped in the office. "My locker partner is the school mascot and she needs more space. I've got to change lockers."

The secretary looked at Ginger suspiciously. "We have one, but the hinge is broken. Otherwise, every locker in the school is being used. Are you sure you can't work something out?"

"I don't mind if the hinge is broken," Ginger answered. "I don't have much stuff."

The woman sighed. "Why don't you come back tomorrow, then. I'll speak to the janitor."

Ginger said that would be okay and bought an apple out of the machine to eat on the front steps. The weather was cold but sunny, and Ginger liked being alone. The sound of water spewing out of the fountain soothed her mixed-up mind.

If it weren't for Rol, she decided, she'd go home after school and skip the dance, but she had promised to go. Somehow she'd have to survive this day. Then what?

Rol Swenson might be the best-looking boy she'd ever met, but she didn't like some of the things he did. And what did it mean to *like* a boy anyway? Did it mean your stomach fell into your shoes whenever you saw him? Or did it mean you really liked him, the way you would feel about your best friend?

After school, Ginger went to the locker room with her costume. Paper bags, hangers, and all sorts of clothes were strewn across the floor as the girls hurried to transform themselves.

No one had mentioned Freman's or the ears all day. What would Doylita say when she saw them? Carefully, Ginger slid everything out of the bag and looked around.

Doylita stood in the corner with two other girls who were helping her wriggle into a long, thin cardboard box, colored yellow, with the words *Juicy-Fruit Gum* printed diagonally across the front. Her white legs danced out the bottom and her arms stuck out of holes on each side of the box. Her eyes peered out through two holes on the front.

Now Ginger could see why she had needed the felt-tip pens. Pretty clever, she thought. She must have restolen the pens; only Doylita would have the nerve.

Shelley dressed up like a skier in a tassled cap, goggles, thick boots, and a long pair of skis. She sat on the bench to hook her bindings.

"How are you going to dance like that?" Ginger asked her.

"I'm not." Shelley tucked her braid into her cap. "This is the perfect costume for someone who can't dance."

A laugh sputtered from Ginger's lips, the first all day.

Corine approached in a beautiful black-and-turquoise Geisha outfit. Her face was chalk-white, with two thick sweeps of eyebrows. "What are you going to be, Ginger?"

The ears and tail still lay in their package on the bench.

"You'll see," Ginger said. She pulled her leotard on over her tights and stretched it up over her shoulders. Then she pinned the pink tail to the back and wiggled a few times.

Corine gasped. "I'd never have the nerve to wear that! Oh, well, Rol should like it."

Ginger examined her costume in the mirror. Maybe it was a little tight. She tried to stretch it down in the back and up in the front. Well, she couldn't help the way she was shaped. She put on her sweater and pulled it across her chest.

"At least you have a good figure," Shelley said. She stood up and inched her way across the scratched old floor beside Ginger, whose silver high heels echoed after her. Shelley's skis turned inward at the toes with each short glide. "I not only can't dance, but I can't ski either. I should have thought of that."

The two made it into the gym and stood next to the wall just inside the door. Myriad kids in a variety of costumes gyrated to music blasting from a stereo system. No one else had come as a bunny.

"Rol said he'd meet me here," Ginger said, adjusting her ears.

Lance Woodward walked up, wearing his usual jeans and hooded sweat shirt. "What are you supposed to be?" he chided.

"I don't know."

"A rabbit or something?"

Ginger looked away. "I can't stand this," she said to Shelley. "I want to go home."

"Not me. I just got all this on. I'm not taking it off until I get my money's worth."

"The dance is free," Ginger said. "We've already gotten our money's worth. See ya." She clomped away without looking back at Lance and melted into a group of kids standing under the basketball hoop.

"Here she is, Rol." Doylita in her gum box bowed her cardboard head. She didn't seem to notice the ears.

A green-skinned vampire in a black tux turned around and looked down at Ginger. Blue eyes peered from between white eyelashes. Fanglike teeth grew out over lips that had been painted with black lipstick. The vampire flung back a satin cape and extended a hand with long, greenish fingernails. "Good evening," he said in a perfect Dracula voice.

Ginger stared. The figure before her looked frightening, even though she knew it was Rol.

"Good evening," she said, shaking the hand.

Doylita started to dance with Carlin Moseby, who had sprayed his hair purple.

"Take off your wrap and stay a while," Rol said in his ghoulish voice.

Ginger laughed nervously as he pulled off her sweater. Automatically her arms wrapped tightly around herself.

"You look bea-u-tiful," Dracula said, looking Ginger up and down. Then he raised his arms to envelope her in his cape.

Ginger coughed. "Excuse me. I can't breathe."

Rol released her, all but one hand, and began to dance across the floor with her.

Ginger noticed Lance leaning against the wall with his thumbs hooked in his pockets. Was she dancing right? Did she look silly? or too naked. She felt the bunny tail wiggle behind her.

Rol nuzzled Ginger's neck annoyingly. She pulled away and wiped the greasepaint from her skin. "Don't," she said, trying to keep her voice cheerful. "I'll turn green."

Funny. Her heart was hardly racing at all, not the way it had when she danced with Rol at the party. Of course, Lance had not been watching her then. She looked up at

Rol. Someone had turned off most of the lights and his make-up glowed in the dark. In the dim light he looked sick, as if he had the flu—or worse.

Ginger braced her elbow against his shoulder and finished the dance at half an arm's length.

22.

A fast song, full of drumbeats followed, then another slow one. Rol moved Ginger backward toward the end wall where it was almost dark. Had he noticed Lance spying on them too? Ginger wondered.

He danced her smoothly into the corner and grinned down at her. Long vampire teeth glowed pale green. Ginger's bunny tail flattened against the brick wall. She barely saw Rol's fingernails move up and take out the teeth, then felt the warmth of his face near hers.

He's going to kiss me, Ginger thought with alarm, and his lips are painted black! She ducked aside just as Rol bent forward and bumped his head on the brick.

"Ouch! Hold still, will you?"

"Sorry." Why did I say that? she wondered. I'm not sorry. I don't want him to kiss me, not now or anytime.

Rol cupped her face tightly in his hands and pressed his lips against hers. Ginger tried to move but was trapped. His entire body seemed to lean on her. The back of her head hit the brick wall. As she tried to escape, she felt her hair grind against the stone, and one bunny ear flopped in front of her face.

"Rol, don't!" She gasped for air.

"What's the matter with you?" he murmured and moved in for another kiss.

His lips seemed to cover her entire mouth, and her nose fought for an open space where she could breathe. She moved her head from side to side, but Rol paid no attention. He went right on kissing, making mumbling noises as if he were eating a candy bar.

Suddenly someone turned on the lights, and Rol's head snapped back.

"Hey!" someone complained.

Lance stood casually a few feet away from the light switches near the main doors, but several other kids stood just as close.

"Who did that? Turn 'em off," Rol ordered.

All eyes seemed to rivet on Ginger and the vampire.

"Look!" A girl pointed and doubled over in hysterical laughter.

Ginger glanced at Rol, whose black lipstick was nearly gone. She clapped her hand to her face. Grease! Even the end of her nose felt slippery. And now the palm of her hand was black, too!

Ginger squirmed, remembering the time her mother had caught her with chocolate frosting on her fingers. "I didn't touch the cake," she had lied, but the truth had been so obvious. Now everyone in the gym knew she'd been kissed. Well, so what? A lot of other kids had been kissing, and no one had paid any attention to them.

Doylita and her yellow box bounced up and down.

Ginger wiped her mouth on her sleeve and looked down with disgust at the greasy, black smudge. Then, hardly able to see, she ran to where she'd left her sweater, picked it up, and hurried toward the nearest door. Her tail wiggled and her ears flopped as she wobbled straight into the boys' locker room.

The door swung shut behind her, and Ginger stood horrified as she realized what she'd done. Boys' shorts and shoes and socks littered the benches along with plastic bags and hangers. Along one wall was a row of urinals.

Ginger rushed past the showers, praying there was another exit the way there was in the back of the girls' locker room. She forced her eyes straight ahead even when she noticed Derrick Johnson wearing only a pair of white socks.

There was another door! Good! She pushed through into the hall. Now to get back to the girls' locker room, grab her clothes, and make a run for the bus. No way was she going back into that dance!

The door behind her opened again, and Rol poked his head out. "What were you doing in here?"

Ginger jumped. "Maybe I was sick."

"Ah, jeez." His voice sounded disgusted, but he stepped out into the hall and wrapped an arm around her.

"Don't!" Ginger said emphatically.

"Hey, I thought we had something going here."

"So did I. I'm sorry . . . really." She folded her arms across her chest and looked at the floor.

"Okay, if that's the way you want it. There are a lot of girls at Alcott. Who needs this?" Dracula snapped his cape back with a flourish.

Ginger took off her mother's shoes and ran along the hall until she found the door marked GIRLS. Safely inside, she pulled her jeans on over her tights and leotard. Her tail bulged in the back, but she didn't have time to take it off.

The ears went quickly into her book bag along with the shoes. She tied on her sneakers and threw her coat over her shoulders, then pushed back through the door into the hallway. Half-expecting Rol still to be waiting for her, she was relieved to find him gone. Now to get outside.

She rushed out the double doors of the school and down the wide stairs. The fountain bubbled soothingly to her left, and she hurried toward it.

Shaking inside, she seated herself on the cold surface of a stone bench. Spray beaded her face, and tears rolled unchecked from the corners of her eyes.

She had once thought kissing Rol Swenson would be so nice, but it wasn't. She hated the way he had pushed her against the wall and trapped her there. Maybe she had asked for it, wearing that tight costume. Rol probably thought she *wanted* to be kissed that way.

I'm only fourteen, Ginger thought defensively. What did Rol expect? He was three years older, after all.

This was all her parents' fault for making her transfer to Alcott. No, that wasn't true. Lance had transferred, too, and he had changed for the *better*. Anyway, Ginger liked her art class, and she liked Shelley. She was beginning to talk to some of the kids in homeroom and was even thinking about trying out for the basketball team. She didn't want to go back to Jefferson now.

"I don't want to go back," Ginger said aloud, surprising herself. Paula and she weren't friends anymore, and she wouldn't know anyone.

Suddenly she felt someone's eyes on her, and she turned with a jerk. Lance stood watching her, his hands in his pockets. He approached Ginger cautiously.

"Hi," he said. "You need a ride home?"

"Oh." Ginger sighed with relief. "It's only you." She wiped her eyes and sniffed. "This dumb fountain—I'm getting drenched."

Lance sat down next to her, looked at the fountain, and looked back at Ginger. "Why don't you move . . . or blow your nose?"

Ginger smiled, but only slightly. "Go away."

"Did I ever tell you about the time I went into the girls' locker room by mistake?"

"You never did that."

"Yes, I did. The boys' and girls' locker rooms were identical, except the showers are on the opposite sides."

Ginger flashed him a look of surprise. "I know," she said and released a long laugh. "Is someone picking you up?"

"Yeah. My mom will be along any minute. She can take you home, too."

"Thanks. I would really appreciate it. Do you think she'll mind?"

"She won't mind." Lance looked closely at Ginger's mouth. "That lipstick looks terrible on you." He reached over and wiped it off with the sleeve of his jacket.

Ginger flushed a little, then relaxed. "I thought I got it all off," she said. "I feel as if I've been tarred. When did you say your mother was coming?"

Lance's face registered a blank. "Oh, well, actually, I. . . ."

"You mean, you haven't really called her? How do you know she'll come?" Ginger sighed with exasperation.

"She will if I ask her." Lance stood up and jumped over the bench. "Just wait right here. I'll only be a minute."

"If the bus comes first, I'm getting on," Ginger warned.

"I'll hurry," Lance said and took off for the school, bounding up the stairs three at a time.

A few minutes later, the bus moaned to a stop at the corner. Impatiently, Ginger glanced toward the school for Lance, saw that he was not coming yet, and got on the bus. She dropped her money into the slot and slid into the front seat next to the window.

The bus pulled away just as a figure came flying out the front doors of the school and down the steps. Ginger turned away. Lance had tricked her. How could he expect her to wait for him?

As the bus rattled past the fountain, Ginger felt Lance looking up at her. Her face flushed as she forced her eyes straight ahead. Well, what else could she do? Soon the dance would be letting out. The school grounds would be crawling with kids, Doylita and Rol included. Ginger had to leave before that.

23.

Ginger stood up. "Wait a minute," she said to the bus driver, "I'm getting off."

"Okay, but I can't refund your fare."

"That's all right." Ginger waited for the doors to yawn open, then hurried down the steps. I can't believe I'm doing this, she said to herself.

Lance, who had started to walk away, turned when the bus stopped again so soon. He smiled in a suspicious kind of way.

"I changed my mind," Ginger said lamely. "I guess I'm not in *that* much of a hurry."

"Guilty conscience?"

"No, pity," Ginger countered.

Lance's brown eyes looked down at her like a scolded puppy.

Ginger waited for his comeback, but he was silent. Finally, she said, "Sorry, that wasn't very nice. I've been doing a lot of things lately that aren't very nice."

"That's okay. I had it coming."

"No, you didn't."

Lance led Ginger back to the bench by the fountain. "Why don't you and I try to be friends." He held out his hand. "Shake?"

"Okay, shake," Ginger said as she clasped his warm hand. It wasn't as large as Rol's, but it felt safer somehow. "Are you the one who turned on the lights in the gym?" she asked as an afterthought.

Lance just smiled.

"I guess I should thank you."

"I told you the guy was a creep."

"How did you know?"

Lance looked deeply into Ginger's eyes and arched one eyebrow. "A man can tell."

Ginger laughed. "You're only fourteen."

"Fifteen," Lance corrected. "What did your parents say when they found out you got caught shoplifting?"

"They don't know about it," Ginger admitted. "And I'm not telling them either. My dad would kill me. He thinks teen-agers are a bunch of sheep anyway."

"You got off pretty easy," Lance said. "Scot free, in fact."

"Yeah, I know. Things don't usually work out that way for me."

Louisa May Alcott stood in the fountain with her gray book, seeming to listen to every word that was said, taking it all down in detail. Ginger turned her back on the fountain. "How long will it take your mom to get here?"

"About twenty minutes." Lance looked at his watch. "Don't worry, the dance won't be over until six-thirty."

"I'm not worried."

"You sure look worried."

As Ginger passed the office Monday morning, Mrs. Ferguson called her in.

"I talked to the janitor about that locker you wanted. He'll try to get the hinge fixed by the time school gets out today. You can move in then if you still want to, but you'll have to share if we get any more new students." She handed her a padlock and card. "Here's the combination."

Ginger looked down at the card. "Thanks," she said. Locker number 24. Another combination to learn.

I'll have to tell Doylita *something*, Ginger thought as she left the office. I can't just disappear without any explanation.

On her way up the creaky stairs she rehearsed in her mind: Doylita, you said yourself this arrangement was only temporary. That's what she could say. And it was even true.

I'll tell her after school as I'm moving out, Ginger decided. That way Doylita wouldn't be able to talk her out of it.

At three o'clock she found the new locker and opened it several times to test the hinges, then snapped on the padlock and tried the combination. It opened easily, now that she knew the system. Ginger paused to take a deep breath before going upstairs to face Doylita.

Why was this so hard? she wondered as she made her way up the stairs. In a few minutes it would be over, and Ginger would no longer be part of Doylita's life.

Rol and Corine appeared above her as they descended the stairs hand in hand. Ginger focused on the point between their arms where their fingers locked together.

Corine's face flushed at the sight of Ginger. Rol grinned smugly.

Don't stare, Ginger scolded herself. Say something. "Have you seen Doylita?"

"I think she went downtown," Corine answered.

"Already? I've got to see her."

Rol and Corine moved down a stair as Ginger continued up. For an instant she stood on the same level with Rol, looking into his eyes. He had no face, Ginger noticed for the first time, just white lashes surrounding blank eyes. He wasn't really handsome at all!

"You can probably catch her if you hurry," Corine went on. "She said she was going to Freman's to get her dad an unbrella. It's his birthday or something tomorrow."

"Oh, okay. Thanks." Ginger continued up the stairs, then stopped short. Umbrella. *Umbrella!* Like a video recording, the scene replayed itself in her mind: she had just left the back room at Freman's and was rushing toward the front doors when Mr. Clarke had stopped her. Again she saw the black fabric snap over his head. "Wanna buy an umbrella?"

Could Doylita have failed to see Mr. Clarke at work

in Freman's? Surely she wasn't so bold as to steal an umbrella right out from under his nose! Mr. Clarke never missed a thing at school; he would catch her for sure!

Ginger stepped up onto the second floor hallway. Two boys brushed past her. The din of metal locker doors opening and closing clamored around her, but she didn't really hear it.

Feelings fought each other in her mind: after all the shoplifting Doylita had done, it would serve her right to get caught finally. On the other hand, this would be Doylita's second trip to the back room; Irene might call the police.

And who could tell? The whole truth might come out, the part about the girls being locker partners. And Ginger had never gotten around to paying the three dollars for the pompons she was still wearing. She could be in more trouble yet. Maybe she hadn't gotten off so free after all.

Ginger's heart began to race. She stood in the middle of the hall with kids bumping into her, feeling faint.

"Hey, you okay?" Lance had been waiting at Ginger's locker and now he rushed toward her.

Ginger looked up. "No . . . not exactly. Doylita's gone downtown for an umbrella. . . ."

"Gee, that sounds serious."

"No, I mean, she's going to *steal* one, and Mr. Clarke sells umbrellas at Freman's."

"Good," Lance said. "Maybe she'll finally get what she has coming to her. No one likes her, you know. They only put up with her because of her dad."

"How do you know?"

"Moseby told me. He thinks she's a pain in the neck,

but he wants to play football. Come on, we're going to miss the bus." He touched Ginger's elbow to guide her back down the stairs.

Ginger thought for a minute. Could it be true? Doylita seemed so popular.

"You mean I was her only friend?"

"You weren't exactly friends, were you?"

"No, I guess not. But you don't understand. I've got to warn her."

"What for? If you're too late, it'll put you at the scene of the crime. Besides, didn't you say you weren't allowed in Freman's anymore?"

"Yes."

"Let's hurry, then. The bus is going to leave in a minute."

Tears glistened in Ginger's eyes, and she couldn't move. Doylita's only friend; she probably thought she could *train* me. What an idiot I've been. Ginger shook the thoughts away. "But if Doylita gets caught. . . ."

"Look, how do you know she isn't going to pay for the umbrella? Or that she won't see Clarke standing there and change her mind?"

Ginger looked into Lance's brown eyes and wanted to believe him. Doylita rarely paid for anything, whether she had money or not. Corine had said she was going to "get" an umbrella, not "buy" one. That meant she was going to rip it off. Still, Lance was right; unless she caught up with Doylita on the sidewalk between the school and Freman's she wouldn't be able to warn her anyway.

"Yeah, okay. I guess there's nothing I can do." Ginger took a deep breath as she started down the stairs with Lance. "She'll notice Mr. Clarke right away," she said, brightening. "He's not exactly the type who blends into the woodwork."

Lance laughed, and Ginger forgot all about moving into her new locker.

24.

The bus stopped inches behind a black-and-white squad car the next morning.

"What are the cops doing here?" one boy asked. "Vandals smash the apple machine again?"

The kids crowded off the bus and gathered on the sidewalk to gape.

Without thinking, Ginger reached for Lance's arm and squeezed it violently. "They're here because of Doylita. I just know it. Or *me*." She could hardly get the last words past the lump in her throat.

"No, they can't be," Shelley said as she patted Ginger's arm. "You took those ears last week. Someone probably stole another typewriter or stuffed toilet paper down the sinks."

Announcements squawked every few seconds from inside the car. Ginger tried but could not make out the messages.

"Relax, will you?" Lance said. "You're cutting off my circulation; not that I mind. . . ."

Ginger let go abruptly. "Sorry. It was just a reflex." She wrapped her collar tightly around her neck as cold air and mist from the fountain worked its way inside her coat.

They hurried up the steps and entered the school.

Something was definitely wrong. It was too quiet, like the time someone had broken into the grade school and stolen the PTA money. A detective had dusted for fingerprints, and everyone acted as if there had been a murder.

Lance noticed, too. He looked around the nearly deserted front hall and through the window into the principal's office.

"Where is everyone?" Shelley whispered.

Ginger looked up at the ceiling and listened intently to the sounds of feet moving around in the upper hall. "It sounds like the whole school is upstairs."

"Let's check it out." Lance led the way up the old wooden steps.

Ginger hurried after him, and Shelley followed, along with a few other kids who had gotten off the same bus. The second floor was glutted with students, all straining to see what was going on. Ginger's locker was in the direction they were looking! Why hadn't she moved her things out the night before? The threesome pushed their way through the crowd until they couldn't move any further.

"What's happening," Lance asked a boy standing in front of him.

"Locker searches."

For a moment Ginger was indignant. Weren't lockers supposed to be private? Then she mentally went over the things she had left on the shelf in 287: some Kleenex, a few old pens and pencils, some school papers, and a book or two; nothing incriminating.

What am I so worried about? she asked herself. Doylita is the one with the "collection" of new merchandise. "What are they looking for?"

"Drugs probably," the boy said.

Another boy turned around "Mr. Wintermeyer called in a cop. They're looking for stolen loot."

The blood seemed to drain from Ginger's face. She raised up on tiptoe and looked over the heads in front of her to see the blue shoulders of a policeman and Mr. Clarke's tan face. The principal was with them, and they all stood in front of locker 287.

"I knew it," Ginger whispered.

"Go on to your homerooms," Mr. Wintermeyer's voice bellowed into the crowd. "This doesn't concern any of you."

A few kids moved, but most of them stayed where they were.

"It's Doyle," someone said.

"What are they hassling her for? She didn't do anything."

How would you know? Ginger wanted to ask.

"Hey, man, she's the school mascot."

So?

The bell peeled out, and the whole crowd jumped as the sound pierced the unusual quiet. Slowly, kids began to walk away.

"Get going," Mr. Wintermeyer urged them.

Ginger stood frozen in one spot. This did concern her. Shelley inched away. "I guess I'd better go. I'll save you a seat at lunch."

Lance stood protectively close to Ginger.

"You don't have to stay," she told him. "It's just that I have to know what's going to happen."

"I'll stay."

As the crowd thinned in front of her, Ginger could see Doylita's small figure leaning against the lockers with her arms folded across her chest. Mr. Willard stood with her, his face red with rage. The policeman held a black umbrella with a wooden handle.

Ginger walked up and stood in front of the group. It was only a matter of time before they asked for her anyway.

Doylita was looking down at the array of things the policeman had lined up on the floor: ball-point pens, thumbtacks, earrings, notecards, a wrench, a box of gumballs, and a thermometer, all still on cards or in their packages.

A dozen or so kids who had remained in the hall whispered among themselves. "I can't believe it," someone said.

"Do you recognize any of these items?" the policeman asked Doylita.

"Nope."

Coach Willard yanked on her arm. "Answer the officer properly."

A mixture of shock and hatred crossed Doylita's face. "No, I don't recognize any of it." Her chin quivered. "It must belong to my locker partner."

Ginger squirmed and clenched her damp hand into a fist.

Lance stiffened beside her. "Tell them," he coaxed her.

The officer straightened. The name Barclay was on his uniform, the name of the sergeant Irene had threatened to call. "Do you know anything about this?"

"It's not mine," Ginger stated simply.

"Then whose is it?"

Ginger looked at Doylita.

"I didn't do anything," Doylita said with a cocky snap to her voice. "In the first place, why would I want any of that junk?"

Her father looked at the ground and shook his head. When he looked up again, his face had changed from anger to pure misery.

"Then, you're saying your locker partner did the stealing."

"Well, she must have." Doylita sounded so sincere. "I know she took some Halloween things once."

"Then how do you explain the umbrella?" He turned it over in his hands until he found a price sticker.

Doylita looked at the floor. After a long silence she mumbled, "I told you, it's mine."

"You never had an umbrella," her father said.

"Do you have sales slips for any of this stuff?" Sergeant Barclay asked.

Doylita didn't answer. Instead, she glared at Ginger as if she ought to take the blame for something she didn't do.

"I think we'd better talk in your office," Sergeant Barclay suggested to the principal.

Mr. Wintermeyer nodded. "Anyone who's not involved, *please* go to your classes."

"I'm sorry, Jesse," Mr. Clarke consoled the coach. "But I thought you'd want to know about this before she gets too involved."

"No, I appreciate it. I had a feeling when I didn't find anything at home that searching her locker might be interesting." His wide shoulders drooped. "What the girl needs is a mother, or at least a full-time father."

At this tears rolled down Doylita's cheeks, and Ginger honestly felt sorry for her.

"You'd better come along, too," Mr. Clarke said to Ginger. "Woodward, go into homeroom and take the roll."

"Yeah, okay," Lance said. He hesitated. "I guess I'll see you at lunch." He touched Ginger's arm.

She watched him walk away. Lance could really be nice when he wanted to, like a good friend. Too bad she had wasted so much time on Rol Swenson.

The group that was left moved solemnly toward the stairs, as if they were heading for a guillotine instead of the principal's office. All eyes were cast to the brown linoleum. Doylita, with her hands clasped in front of her, walked without the slightest bounce or wiggle to her hips. Even her hair, Ginger noticed, hung straight down her back.

Sergeant Barclay carried a plastic bag full of Doylita's "collection." "The price tags are all coded," he explained. "Most of this merchandise came into the store in September, so it's all been stolen since school started."

"Will charges be pressed?" Coach Willard wanted to know.

"The case will be referred to juvenile court," Sergeant Barclay said.

Ginger hurt inside, thinking of her own father and how he'd feel if he ever found out about the bunny ears.

25.

Her own chin felt on the verge of quivering as she turned to Mr. Clarke. "I took some bunny ears before Halloween, but I got caught and gave them back," Ginger told him. "It's the only time in my life I ever stole anything, and I'm never going to do it again." For some

144

reason it was important that Mr. Clarke understand. "I didn't take any of that stuff in the locker."

"I didn't think you did." Mr. Clarke kept his arms folded across the front of his red sweater, as if he were as nervous as Ginger.

The door opened, and Miss Stanley came into the office wearing a pair of gray warm-ups. "Jesse, I just heard about the trouble. . . ."

Doylita suddenly jumped to her feet. "I'm not staying if she's going to be in here! Get her out of here!" Her voice cracked, out of control.

Miss Stanley sobered as if someone had slapped her face. Her mouth opened, and she turned to the coach.

Mr. Willard stood up and put an arm around Miss Stanley. "Sit down!" he ordered Doylita. "I'll tell you when you can leave. Marge is only trying to help."

"I don't need any help," Doylita snapped. "I took the umbrella for *you*." The confession out, she stopped herself.

Everyone in the office quietly stared at Doylita. She's trapped herself, Ginger thought. Maybe her life isn't so perfect after all.

"Fine birthday present," Coach Willard mumbled.

Doylita's large blue eyes opened wide as she looked desperately from one person to the next. "That is . . . what I meant was. . . ." Slowly she sat down again.

Sergeant Barclay shifted his bulky weight and took charge in an official-sounding voice. "Are you aware that shoplifting is a serious crime?" he asked.

"Yes," Doylita whispered.

"This incident could become part of your permanent record."

"You took the other things, too, didn't you?" Coach Willard asked.

Doylita dropped her head in silence.

"Didn't you!" he demanded.

"Jesse, be gentle with her," Miss Stanley said. "She's only looking for a little attention."

"That's a fat lie," Doylita cried.

"Well, it's not going to work. There are other ways to get attention." Coach Willard turned to the others. "Look, I'm really sorry about this. I'll see that every last item is returned or paid for." He spoke mainly to Sergeant Barclay.

She'll never be able to shop in Freman's again, Ginger thought.

At lunch the whole school buzzed with speculation about Doylita. Would they take her to juvenile hall? Would she have to go to court? What was her father going to do about her?

Doylita was not with her usual group as Ginger quietly passed by and headed for the far side of the cafeteria.

"I've ripped off a few things, too," she heard Corine say. "Hasn't everyone? Who would have thought they'd actually come to the school and search the lockers?"

"I'm going through my locker after lunch," Rol Swenson said. "No telling what's still lying around in there. I would have done it this morning, but I couldn't get through the hall."

Ginger pretended not to notice them and went to sit with Shelley and Lance.

"Tell us what happened." Shelley looked up through her round glasses. "Every detail."

"Poor Doylita. She's really in a lot of trouble."

146

"Poor Doylita, nothing. You're off the hook, aren't you?" Lance really looked concerned.

"Yeah, I'm off the hook, but I should have moved out of the locker yesterday the way I was supposed to."

"But this way you have the inside story," Shelley said. "Come on, tell us what happened."

"I don't really know much, except that Doylita admitted she took the umbrella. Her dad was really mad. Miss Stanley was the only one who was nice to her, and Doylita tried to order her out of the room. She and the coach must be going together or something."

Several other kids at the table were listening. "I heard they're getting married," an Oriental girl put in.

"I think Miss Stanley's nice," Shelley said. "She'd be a good stepmother."

"Doylita will throw a fit," Ginger said, and she stared off into space while voices continued to hum around her. And she had thought she had problems. Transferring to a new school was nothing. At least she had her family and friends. What would she do if her dad suddenly got married again? If she didn't have a mother?

"Hey," Lance called. "Are you listening? I said, we'll help you switch lockers, if you want."

"Oh . . . okay. Thanks," Ginger said. "To tell you the truth, I'm not very hungry. Anyone want this?" She pushed her lunch tray toward the middle of the table.

"Hamburger gravy on fake potatoes; you've got to be kidding," Lance said. "Let's go." He followed Ginger and Shelley out of the cafeteria. "It'll be weird passing your locker in the basement from now on. You won't forget which one you're in, will you?"

"If I do, I'm sure you'll be around to remind me," Ginger quipped.

Approaching locker 287, she saw Doylita standing with Ellen Warneke. Trying to recruit a new trainee already, Ginger thought. But Doylita seemed to be moving out of the locker before Ginger had the chance.

Doylita's things were piled on the floor, including the boots to her cougar outfit. Ellen was transferring everything to paper bags.

Ginger approached cautiously, stopping several feet from the locker. Doylita glanced in her direction but didn't seem to see her. Her eyes were red-rimmed, and she looked dazed as she set each item on the floor.

"I can't believe your dad's doing this to you," Ellen said. "Maybe we could get up a petition."

Doing what to her? Ginger looked at Lance and then at Shelley.

"I'm not going to any school out in the sticks," Doylita said. Her voice quivered.

"You'll have to ride the bus," Ellen sympathized. "You won't get home until after dark." She thought for a minute. "Jefferson has a lousy football team. Maybe he'll change his mind."

"No, he won't." Doylita sniffed loudly and tossed her hair behind her shoulder. "*Mar-jor-ie* think it's a good idea."

Jefferson? Doylita was being transferred to Jefferson!

Lance had heard, too, and muffled a laugh.

Doylita looked up. "If it isn't Miss Goody-two-shoes." She stared at Ginger for a long moment, and sparks of hatred danced in the space between.

Ginger felt as if her heart had fallen into her stomach. "I want to know one thing, Doylita. Why did you tell them I took all that stuff?"

Doylita turned back to her locker as if she felt no guilt at all. "A *real* friend would have stuck by me."

Dumbfounded, Ginger did not respond at first. Even Ellen looked at Doylita oddly.

"You mean, I was supposed to stick by you while you lied about me? That doesn't make much sense."

Shelley laughed.

"I *am* the school mascot."

No one answered. They all gaped at Doylita.

Ellen Warneke dropped a few more things into a paper bag and said, "Finish this yourself. I've got to go." She walked off without even saying good-bye.

"So, go!" Doylita called after her. "I don't care about you, or anybody else!" Fresh tears dampened her cheeks.

Ginger took a step forward. She wanted to touch Doylita's shoulder but changed her mind. "Look, it won't be so bad. Jefferson is okay. I could introduce you to a friend of mine who still goes there."

"Gee," Doylita sneered. "That would really be swell."

Ginger ignored the sarcastic remark. "I don't think they have a mascot. Maybe you could talk to the coach."

Doylita forced a high-pitched laugh. "And be a cowgirl? No way!"

"Well, it's just a suggestion. I think you'd be perfect in a red-and-white fringed skirt and a western hat. You could pull the fur off your white boots and. . . ."

"I said no, okay? So just leave me alone."

The bell rang, ending the lunch period. "Come on," Lance said. "You're wasting your time."

"Well, good-bye," Ginger said.

Doylita did not even look up as the threesome turned

and walked away. You'd think nothing ever bothered Doylita, Ginger thought, but it did.

"See you around," Doylita finally called, and Ginger looked back long enough to wave. There was really nothing else to say.

Walking back down the hall with her friends, Ginger felt an unexpected sadness. She was glad she wouldn't have to listen to any more of Doylita's weird ideas or to her bossy tone of voice, but Alcott school would never be the same again. The games and pep assemblies wouldn't be as much fun without the small blond cougar. No one would ever be able to do it as well as Doylita had.

"I guess there's not much point in moving out of the locker now," Ginger said. "I'd better go tell Mrs. Ferguson in the office."

"I'll go with you," Shelley offered.

Lance walked with them. "You know, you were too nice to her after what she did to you."

"Maybe. I don't know." Guilt niggled at the edges of Ginger's mind. She had shoplifted, too, but nothing like this had happened to her.

They walked on in silence to the office. "Somehow I can't picture Doylita at Jefferson," Lance said, holding the door open for the two girls.

"I can." Ginger laughed. "She'll have the school turned upside down within a week. Wait till Paula gets a load of Doylita Willard."

26.

Three weeks later, near the end of November, Ginger stretched out on her bed and luxuriated in the knowledge that her room was perfectly tidy for the first time since she had transferred to Alcott. She had always kept her room spotless in the old days, when Paula was coming over almost every day after school; but this fall, until now, she hadn't cared about the mounds of dirty socks or her unmade bed.

It was weird how things had worked out. She had to admit she did miss Doylita at school, the lively way she bounced when she walked, the way she laughed, and the way she always seemed to be at the center of school activities. Maybe if she was good the rest of the year at Jefferson, her dad would let her come back to Alcott for her sophomore year.

And Irene, the woman from Freman's, had probably been right; Ginger was lucky to have gotten caught the first time she took something. At least she hadn't been tempted to try it again.

Ginger looked lazily out her window at the grayish lavender sky. On a cold day like this, the only thing she wanted to do was enjoy the coziness of her own bedroom.

As she gazed trancelike through the panes, tiny white specks formed out of the grayness, little flakes that drifted downward past the squares of her window.

A whoop sounded from the adjacent room. "It's snowing!" Mark screamed. "Hey, Ginger, it's snowing!"

Ginger was already at the window. Against the bare

trees outside, she could see that snowflakes did indeed fill the sky.

Her spirits took a giant leap. Oh, I hope it sticks, she caught herself thinking. By nightfall they could have enough for sledding.

Mark burst into her room.

"Can't you knock?" Ginger complained automatically. "Oh, never mind. It's okay. Come on in."

Mark rushed to the window, a huge smile on his face. "I hope my boots still fit," he said, rubbing his palms together in anticipation.

As they watched the snow together, the tiny flakes turned into loose pats of cotton that nearly obliterated the house across the street.

"Look, the lawn is almost covered!" Ginger exclaimed.

"Maybe the lights will go out, the way they did last winter, and we'll have to make popcorn in the fireplace. Do you think the lights will go out?"

"They will if the wires get too heavy with snow."

Mark did not question her authority. "I wonder where my flashlight is."

Ginger watched him bound from her room. Mark wasn't so bad most of the time, especially when they were alone together. She was glad that his Furry Burry wasn't still lying outside behind the bushes. A bear could get ruined in weather like this.

Ginger followed him downstairs to the laundry room. "Come on, let's go out and make a snowman," she suggested.

"You really want to . . . with me?"

"Sure, it'll be fun." Ginger put on a red-and-blue ski jacket, pushed her feet into a pair of high boots, and pulled a white knitted cap down over her ears.

Mark stomped his feet into his boots, and together he and Ginger trudged outside into a blast of frigid air.

Ginger smiled into the white sky, letting snowflakes land on her tongue and eyelashes.

Mark scooped a handful of snow off the top of the garbage can and squeezed it into a ball. "It packs great," he said and wound up to pitch the ball across the street.

Lance Woodward, speeding toward them on his bicycle, ducked just as the snowball sailed over his head.

"Hey, watch it!" Lance hollered and pulled into the yard, leaving a tire track in the fresh snow. His nose and ears were scarlet.

Mark dropped his arms to his sides. "Oops, sorry."

"Hi," Ginger said.

Lance cupped his hands and blew warm air onto his fingers. "Guess what? I've just been down to the school."

"You mean Jefferson?"

"No, Alcott."

"You rode your bike all the way to Alcott? What for?"

"If you'll shut up a minute, I'll tell you." Lance reached over and pulled Ginger's cap over her eyes. "The fountain froze last night. It's nothing but a mound of ice."

"You're kidding." She pulled the cap off and rearranged her hair. She could clearly picture the stone lady with icicles hanging from her chin and elbows.

"Wintermeyer forgot to turn it off, and the pipes burst."

"I love it!" Ginger squealed. "I hope it's ruined."

"The principal and maintenance man are both there trying to decide what to do about it. If it costs too much to fix, they're going to turn the fountain into a planter next spring."

A smile spread across Ginger's face. "That's a great idea, as long as they don't plant Scotch broom."

Lance seemed too cold to get the joke. He pushed his hands momentarily into the front of his jacket, then took them out again and leaned forward on his bike. "Well, I'd better get going."

"Wait. Why don't you come on in and have some hot chocolate. My mom already has some made."

Lance looked down at his blue-jeaned legs. "I'm kind of wet."

"That's okay. You can leave your pants in the laundry room."

"Very funny."

Mark smashed a snowball into the trunk of a bare maple tree. "I knew it! You aren't going to build any snowman with me!"

"Yes, I am," Ginger said with a sigh. "We can do it later. The snow will probably be better by then, anyway."

"Later means never." Mark folded his arms across his chest.

"Tell you what," Lance said. "Why don't you bring the chocolate outside. I'll help your brother with his snowman."

"You don't have to do that," Ginger insisted.

Mark smiled broadly. "He can if he wants."

Ginger went into the house, stomping snow off her boots on the back porch. "I'm going to take some hot chocolate outside, if that's okay."

"That's fine." Mrs. Wilson was standing at the kitchen sink looking out the window. "New friend?"

"Oh, that's Lance Woodward. He transferred with me from Jefferson."

154

"He looks like a nice boy."

"He is." Ginger stood beside her mother and looked out. Lance and Mark were rolling a huge ball of snow. Bits of grass and dirt clung to the sides. Ginger smiled. "Don't you remember him? He's that grubby kid who used to chase me home from school."

"Looks to me as though he's still chasing."

"Mom! He's just a friend." Was he? Ginger wondered. She turned to the stove and stirred the steaming cocoa. There were so many things she'd like to tell her mother, about Lance and Rol Swenson and Doylita, but. . . .

Mrs. Wilson took three mugs out of the cupboard. "You know, it's less than a month until Christmas, and I haven't even started my shopping. The snow gets me in the mood."

Ginger's ears seemed almost to stretch toward her mother as she held each mug over the sink and poured it full of hot chocolate. Mrs. Wilson dropped in some marshmallows.

"Mark wants a computer. Freman's has one on sale this week." Mom arranged the full mugs on a tray and added a package of graham crackers.

Ginger's heart lurched.

"Why don't you and I go shopping this afternoon?"

Ginger picked up the tray and turned away from her mother. Her hands shook so badly that the mugs skidded across the tray and knocked into each other. Was this a trap? Did her mother already know that she couldn't go into Freman's?

"Careful there," Mom said. "Well, what do you think? We could have lunch and then hit Freman's before it gets too crowded."

"Well . . . sure. It sounds like fun, except. . . ."
Except what? Ginger's armpits started to itch and then to trickle. "I sort of wanted to build a snowman with Lance."

Mrs. Wilson smiled. "You mean you'd rather be with a cute boy than your boring old mother."

Ginger turned and forced a laugh. "Yeah, do you mind?"

"No, I guess not. Maybe we can go tomorrow."

Ginger drew in her breath and steadied the tray, then she pushed open the back door. Shopping with her mother! She hadn't considered that until now. What would she do? Mrs. Wilson loved Freman's. It was the best department store in town. Ginger's school clothes were bought there every year. She supposed in time she would change enough so that people wouldn't recognize her, but for the next few years. . . .

Mark did a sliding ski-stop in front of the back steps. Curls of steam rose from each mug as Ginger held out the tray. The brown liquid sloshed back and forth. Ginger stared down at it and thought about her sentence. There was no way to keep it a secret. She would have to tell her mother and then, of course, her father would find out, too. She looked deep into the chocolate, and her stomach turned inside out.

How could I be so stupid! For a second she forgot she was holding the tray, and the next thing she knew Mark was yelling at her and the snow at her feet was speckled with brown spots.

Lance bent down to pick up the mugs. "You okay? You looked kind of dizzy or something."

Ginger swallowed. "I . . . I'm sorry. I'll get some more."

"What happened?" Mrs. Wilson appeared at the back door.

"She dumped the whole tray in the snow," Mark said, sounding like his old self again.

"I *said* I would get some more. OKAY?" Ginger picked up the tray, collected the mugs from Lance and followed her mother back into the house.

"Mom, could I talk to you for a minute?"

"Sure. Is something bothering you, honey? Here, let me get you some clean mugs." She reached high into the cupboard for three Santa cups that hadn't been used since last year.

Ginger didn't know where to begin. If only there were some way to tell the story so she didn't sound so *guilty*.

"My locker partner . . ." she started. "No, the fountain. . . ." She cleared her throat to try again. "What would you say if I told you someone I know got caught shoplifting at Freman's?"

Mrs. Wilson set the cups down on the counter slowly, one by one, and when she turned around her face was very serious.

"Who?"

Ginger couldn't bear to answer, and she stood staring at her mother until she felt the wetness of tears on her cheeks.

"Was it you?" her mother asked solemnly.

Ginger's throat tightened so that she could hardly speak. "Please don't hate me."

Mrs. Wilson refilled the mugs and took two of them to the back door. When she returned she said, "I guess we'd better have a talk." She didn't smile, just looked at Ginger with the same kind of misery that had been on

Coach Willard's face when he found out what Doylita had done.

"I never meant to take anything," Ginger began. She closed her eyes and forced her mind into a happier place. For just a moment she was at school, sitting on the stone bench beside Louisa May Alcott. Mist from the fountain dampened her face, and Lance sat next to her with one arm draped around her shoulder.

Too bad you couldn't know the ending to a story in the beginning, Ginger thought. She would have made this one come out different.

She pulled out a kitchen chair and sat down across from her mother.